THE ART OF THE KNOCK

THE ART OF THE KNOCK

STORIES
by Philip Graham

William Morrow and Company, Inc.
New York

I would like to express my gratitude to The MacDowell Colony for its hospitality during the summers of 1982 and 1983. My special thanks to Raymond Bongiovanni and Maria Guarnaschelli for their faith and support.

The author is grateful for permission to reprint stories that appeared, sometimes in slightly different form, in the following magazines: *Carolina Quarterly* ("Ancient Music"), *Fiction Network, Providence Journal,* and *The Washington Post Magazine* ("Twins"), *The Greensboro Review* ("The Deserted House"), *Hampden-Sydney Poetry Review* ("The Distance"), *Mid-American Review* ("I Dreamt About You Last Night" and "Through the Binoculars"), *New Virginia Review* ("The Road to China"), *The New Yorker* ("Light Bulbs"), *Skyline* ("China"), *Some* ("Shadows"), *Sun Dog* ("Stan and Patty"), *Unmuzzled Ox* ("Silence"). "Waiting for the Right Moment" will appear in *River Styx* after publication.

The illustrations for "Silence" are from *Catchpenny Prints: 163 Popular Engravings from the Eighteenth Century Originally Published by Bowles and Carver* (New York: Dover Publications, Inc., 1970).

Library of Congress Cataloging in Publication Data

Graham, Philip, 1951–
    The art of the knock.

    I. Title.
PS3557.R217A88   1985   813'.54   84-11584
ISBN 0-688-04117-5

Printed in the United States of America

First Edition

1 2 3 4 5 6 7 8 9 10

BOOK DESIGN BY SUSAN HOOD

For Alma,
once more

Contents

Contents

THE ART OF THE KNOCK

I

The Road to China

We seem to have been digging for a very long time. Everything gets darker, and darker, and while with our shovels the path constantly gives way, it never breaks into a clearing. We feel like a huge pin attempting to burst the most recalcitrant balloon.

So we continue to grope our way through this ever-retreating unwelcoming party: the rocks scream insults at our tools, their newborn children make sharp comments at our heels, the dirt dissembles, is evasive to our every question, and the worms conduct twisted investigations of our air. In fact, we are forever being opportuned by worms, and we are forever cutting their curiosity in half.

Lunch break. We love lunch. All we ever eat is lunch, three lunches a day: lunch lunch lunch. Ham and cheese on white bread. At least, that's what our tongues tell us— it's difficult to see. When you've come as far as we have, you can eat what you please. However, as we chew, we mull over the deeply felt absence of whole wheat. We wash it down with coffee.

We pick up our shovels and return to this dark door we always open and yet remain outside of. We chip away at what we hope to be behind it: the possibility of an exotic marketplace, intrigue and its attendant court, intense voices that reject our alphabet. We long for watercress, peonies, a bed of rice.

We sleep. We dream of bamboo and its roots that, in their own quiet ways, are growing to greet us. We dream of strange rituals that slowly transform into the familiar, each gesture just on the edge of being translated. But mostly we dream of erosion: we dream we are two clouds pouring ourselves into the retreat of earth. Sleep has become just like work, only with our eyes closed, because when we wake we find we have clawed our way even farther through the tunnel face. After yawning, exhausted, we turn back several yards to retrieve our tools. We pretend nothing has happened and begin our habitual argument. You moved the shovels. No, you did.

These dull tools. After all our careful and devoted sharpening, all they do is shrink away. Soon they'll be nothing but exposed necks, wooden phrases against this hard silence. The tunnel is returning the compliment: it begins to wear us away. Yet if we're lucky, if we're really lucky, we'll end up scraping our hands—our shovels long gone—against the first root tips, those same root tips that have been growing toward us for such a long time.

II

The Art of the Knock: One

First rule: don't deny the knock its pleasure, *play* with it. You can tap with gentle beckoning, pound with a cast of thousands, or rap out the first few bars of your favorite piano concerto—anything to attract the proper attention. It depends on what you're selling. Me, I sell anything, and so I'm an adaptive knocker.

I especially go in for novelties. The Dissolving Toothpick. A fine piece of merchandise, effective on even the hardcore content: you're about to home in on that tiny but individualistic shred of meat when your pick disappears into a popular minty aftertaste. Now to move a product like this, I've developed the *antiknock*. I rap very forcefully, stopping just a half-inch shy of the door. It's a talent and requires concentration. I've been known to terrify a door with implied threats for hours while waiting for the residents to chance out on an errand. It may startle them at first, but then they admire my dedication. And when they see the logic between my delivery and my inventory, well, I sell a lot of dissolving toothpicks.

Another item: the All-Peel Orange. Nothing but peel, this admirable citrus attraction will fatigue even the hardiest fingernail. Now I knock with a roll of the knuckles, a sound that resembles your desire as you rip into an orange. And when the door opens I follow it, alternating between two knuckles a short rap that assumes the scent of rind as the blood puzzles beneath your fingertips. Again, it's logic. You see, I *gladly* give away the itch; it's the scratch I sell. And so All-Peel Oranges are a hot number. So hot that sometimes I've been forced to sell juice oranges as All-Peels.

And that's another rule: always display your honesty as if it were stemware shining under a bright light and then point out the little crack of deceit in each one. This relaxes your customers. They think they don't have to watch so carefully when you're being open about your misrepresentation, and when you've got them in that frame of mind you can really begin to omit details or stretch the short tale long.

It's all part of knowing your customer. If I've been relieved of a dozen Beanless Bags by a bald man, I approach his particular desert with sand in my shoes: for I happen to have in my suitcase . . . the Toothless Comb. Its frame fits to the curve of his head; its absent teeth leave no furrows. Perhaps the breeze of his arm, reliving an almost forgotten yet familiar occupation, will awaken the tiny hair buds that lie dormant on the snowy plain of the skull. Because *everything* is a season, and these truths, and these lies, who's to say which sheds the other? I'm open-minded. I'm willing to believe there's no difference between them: it just depends what side of the door you're on. And not only what side, but the door itself, what disguise it assumes. When I work a street I see them lined up, posing on the face of the house as a loose tooth, a gag in the mouth, or even a mouth that opens into a great sob.

None of this fools me or my knock. Even up close I've

come to know the tiniest impersonations of doors. Their coarse, grainy faces lie and weave into such childish pictures: shoots urging to the surface, a rocket's trail, or ants speeding through the sand. I simply stare impassively, knowing each door for what it is—a *map*. And I'm ready to travel. So I don't gawk at the facade, I follow it: my knuckles become feet and I find myself trudging through the mud after a hard rain; I see off the road a chimney through the trees. I smell the smoke, the dogs smell me, and the growling cranks up. Perhaps I'll sell Dog Chewies in the shape of muzzles . . . or, as I see the glint of rifle, perhaps I'll sell Chocolate Bullets with fruit fillings. . . . Or perhaps in the middle of this story the door I'm knocking on will open. The occupant doesn't wait to ask me what road my knuckles were traveling—he doesn't care!—he just slams the door shut. I pause a few moments, the bones of my face resting against this plank that once, long ago, screamed hello to a ripsaw.

It's a rough life, I don't deny it. If you're in the business you learn to inhale indifference, exhale extenuating circumstances. You learn to seek out towns that lock their doors but keep their windows open. Most important, you learn to avoid those towns where doors have *hands* instead of knobs. Because even after a beautiful knock, it's fifty-fifty who'll get a grip on whom.

That is, *if* your knock is worth *anything*. For those hands may fist themselves asleep into a knob, but get close enough and they'll wake and stretch to fingers, the palms reared back as if to pounce. How can you concentrate? If you begin with a polite pound, that hand half-closes as if, bored, it's examining its nails. If you increase to staccato beat, it turns and taps *its* fingers against the door, ruining your rhythm. And—ha!—if you trick it and switch to ragtime and turn its tapping contrapuntal, the hand, furious as a small child, reaches out, grasps you by the belt, and shakes your triumph out of you. And should a voice inside shout, "Come on in," just try and open the door. You'll have to hand-wrestle, and it can even lead to worse: once I had a knob pull a knife on me!

I returned to this town, bitter, selling Fiberglass Gloves. I wasn't halfway down my first block when a knob, gun in hand, menacingly motioned me away. Well, I believe in ventilation and I never contradict trajectory, so I took the hint and left in a hurry while behind me every door shook its fist in rage. . . .

Oh, I do have my troubles, but I just pass them on to the consumer. Sometimes without even trying. Once I was stuck with a batch of scrawny canaries—all beak and not enough feathers to make a respectable duster. I couldn't sell them. So I *gave* them away—with each purchase of Super-Grow Birdy Vittles. I sold the whole bunch at a rest home, the windows full of lonely old women squinting out at the passing traffic. All I needed was a pathetic little knock that could *almost* expire on the door—I knew the old girls would go for that. How could I have predicted what that bird chow would do? I didn't suspect. I was even surprised when the next time I passed the old home—oddly in disrepair—an enormous bird stared out from each window, feathers luxurious and beaks fat with a cruel, blue sheen. . . .

That was the last time I tried to sell anything *there*. In this trade you've got to keep moving to new territory. And once there, experiment with your knock, find better ways to coax a door open. Me, I recognize an innovation by the way the hinges hum along with my knuckles, creating a lovely duet that begs for three-part until the sound of approaching footsteps completes the harmony. The door opens and a face that could burn a hole through a safe-deposit box smiles chasms through my pathetic patter until I'm lost in a blind alley of bronzed promises, stale flowers of speech—my entire catalog of embroidery. And it all drops to the floor when she asks, "Do you carry any miracles?"

I immediately reply that I've been burdened with miracles for months with no market in sight.

"Until now," she says.

I spread before her my wares, beginning with the *economy-size miracle* of freshly baked wrists that rise to an aroma of hands with curling fingers. Her sniffs beg for more and so I unravel the *medium miracle* of the nape of the neck with its burst of forest and my tongue that rains. Her pores blossom into my *jumbo miracle* of her back and its bone-train that choochoos into my heart. She derails my restraint and I lie on my side with the *king-size miracle* of the curve of her belly as if the world or my eyes were turning. And, as we unfold the *comprehensive miracle* of the perpetual leap of legs, an angry voice suddenly begins banging on the door. Being an expert at knocks, I know when to cut short a sales pitch and seek out the nearest window.

You can never be sure when a product will backfire. Before you know it, very recent customers are exercising their constitutional rights by chasing you down the street! Once or twice I've been holed up in a rainy barn with the howls of a dog pack drawing closer. I just wait for the Chili-Pepper Doggy Bones I seem to have misplaced to take their effect.

In spite of it all, I still dream of the perfect knock. Obsessed, I seek the addition that makes this bundle of ones a five-spot that'll bribe entry anywhere, the handy music that steadily climbs to a bolero and then rips into a breakdown! Oh, I can play the door into a square dance, rumble a rumba, rat-a-tat a tango. You see, my knock is both music *and* dance, both grace notes and gambol: a hubbub of arpeggios that hoof it on this grainy cabaret!

Yet if my customers greet my euphonious measures with catcalls and whistles so that all my knocks end up syncopating the blues, *no problem*—perfection pounds in many guises. For my knock is also any card game you can imagine and I'm always dealt the best hand. My fist can be a royal flush or a tidy trump. Why stop with cards? *Any game.* My fingers are checkers that shout, *King me;* in a huddle they plot the next touchdown; as a fist they bowl down every street for a strike.

But while the perfect game lurks in every door, I haven't pitched it yet. Still, I keep banging around, searching for clues. So what if I'm tagged out attempting to steal? So what if my bluff is called? So what if a dog fouls me? Even if my delivery goes into overtime, or I'm down to my last play with ten more yards to go, or I strike out, or I feint and parry for days without an opening—*I don't care.* Because each door is a domino and all I have to do is find the right order. If not today, no matter. *They'll all fall.*

Silence

Around here, we have banished the voice. Too messy, too much ease of misinterpretation, too much mumble, hiss, and shout. No, we have retained for the mouth its true, original function as receptacle, not cannon bore. Why, our children, when we tell them of speech, can only conceive of it as a kind of clear and noisy vomit.

Another means of communication seems to us far better: as we write, so do we "speak"; we have chosen the ten strong throats attached to our hands. We love how their words travel yet at the same time stay. How they never shed a skin to an echo. How, clear to sight, rather than tell a lie our hands remain stuffed in pockets. And so even immobile, the bulge of deceitful intent belies itself, becomes a confession.

But out in the air our hands orchestrate a wind of words. Imagine every stormy branch in summer telling tales, and only then can you begin to see how we converse. Of course we are proud: who else has an alphabet that twists sound into dance? With such silent steps we reveal ourselves, and receive: the tips of our fingers now antennae.

Yet not all is well. Granny only knits, all day. Yet produces nothing, because in anger we have taken away her yarn. Our children at times are still curious about this and try to decipher what she is saying. We tell them Granny is an immigrant and speaks another language. Grandpop is arthritic and therefore mute. And he never dares to use his voice, for in the past when Granny made such attempts we rewarded her with more than one slap across the mouth, which means "silence":

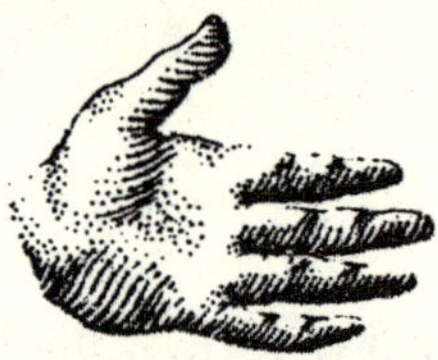

Occasionally at these moments Grandpop would look as if to laugh, but the single word "beware"

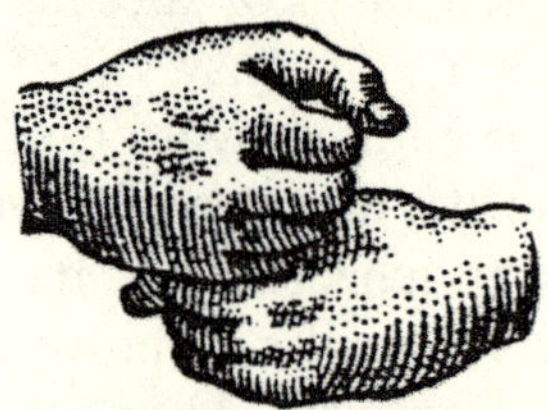

quickly withered that idea. Granny has, however, learned one sign:

meaning "I want." When our children were first born, she hovered above their cradles, under our watchful eyes, repetitiously gesticulating until they had learned their first lesson in language:

Now, after making her one sign, Granny will silently move her lips, designating her desire. We feign ignorance and, as always, she is reduced to pointing.

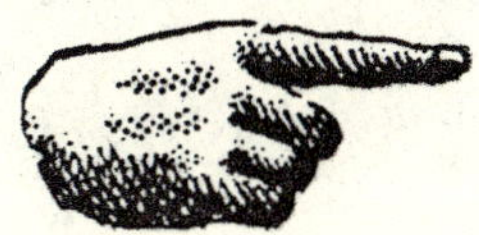

Our children watch these exchanges with fear, seeing, they think, the senility to which we shall all be subject. And so they cry, spreading their fingers from their eyes down the full length of their cheeks.

Our children. We watch with pride as our children gaily stroke each other with their word games, excitedly brush and pat to each other their secrets. But most of all, we love it when, hands flailing overhead, they sing:

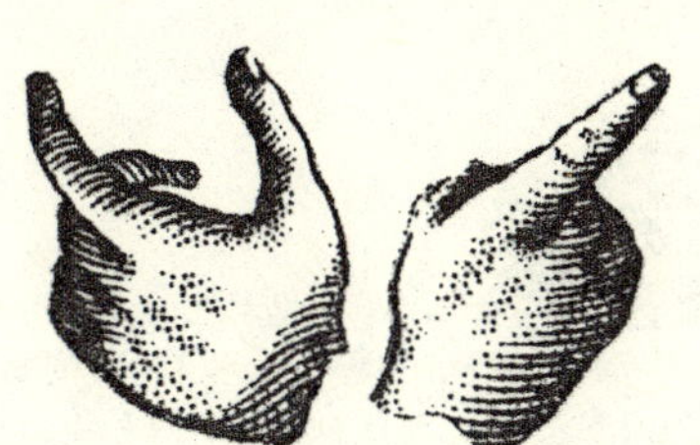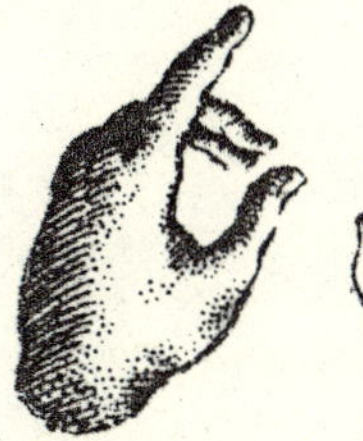

Yet lately, they keep to themselves. Many times we have entered their room, only to have them abruptly turn around to face us, their hands twitching behind their backs. More and more, we don't understand the words they use, and we are not convinced of their explanations.

Their only reply to our doubts is four hands, held limply on the surface of the table.

Because Granny and Grandpop refuse to, or cannot, speak, and because our children increasingly refuse to speak clearly to us, my wife and I spend a great deal of time alone. At night, side by side, we whisper:

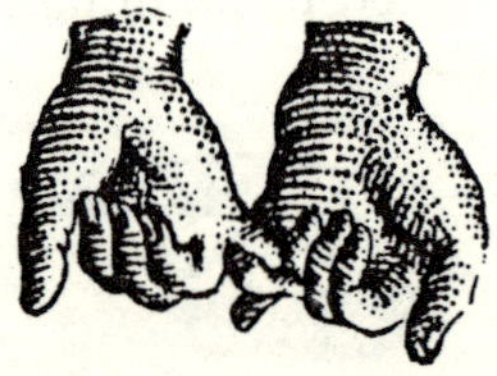

Telling our secrets of the day to each other has become our own private fondling,

until soon our words rub into desire:

Yet we are careful not to have children. Not that we don't care for our first two. But something always stops us, even in the most intense tumble of passion. While in the room next door, brother and sister together snore by scrubbing their sweaty palms against the wooden sideboards of the bed.

Through the Binoculars

I was a young girl when I first found the binoculars. My father was away at work, my mother was somewhere down the block, and I was alone in the house systematically walking from room to room, touching all the furniture I wasn't allowed to touch. I was in my parents' bedroom, surveying all the defenseless, forbidden objects, when I saw my father's binoculars on the bureau. I approached them and saw my double image in the lenses peering back at me, closer and closer. Then my small hands were around the scopes, heavy when I lifted them to my eyes, as if two of me *were* inside. Instead there was the striped design of my parents' pillows—something else not to touch—at first blurry but then as clear as I'd ever seen it. I rushed to the attic, to the window where I knew I could see everything; I searched for my mother but she was nowhere in sight. Instead I watched the faces that walked by the streets: distracted, worried, blank, or angry. They were all unaware of me, because they didn't have binoculars. How safe I felt, seeing and not being seen in return.

I found myself returning to the attic every day. Nothing was exempt from my curiosity. It was summer, and one weekend the carnival arrived. I observed it for hours, patiently waiting for my parents to take me. When they finally did I knew every ride and stall by heart and I effortlessly led them, unbelieving, down each alley as if I lived another life. During weekends I watched the park and the young men and women who held hands, caressed, and vanished among the foliage—mysterious actions that somehow beckoned to me. One evening I made out my parents' car returning from a party. I could see it clearly, even down to the license plate, as it wobbled and lurched home and I first realized my father was becoming an alcoholic. After that my respect for binoculars grew: they revealed what was delightful and also what was not.

At the same time I became fascinated by the mechanics of it all, just how many turns of the thumb and forefinger it would take to focus in on the leaves of the maple across the street. There was something pure about the way the two lenses agreed on the distance between them, so that everything in their path could become clearer and larger. And I felt inside that if distant people could grow before my eyes, then someday I would too. When I'd memorized every corner of the neighborhood from my bedroom window, I began to train the binoculars elsewhere. I'd passed by the dried flowers in the hallway so many times, but the view through the binoculars from the top of the stairs showed me, in every sad and fragile feature, the little world it had always been. I discovered that the kitchen spoons shone because of the passing light and not from any inner quality; I saw a still life even in the folds of a discarded Kleenex. And as my parents argued, I saw the bluff in my father's jaw, and that when angry my mother's eyes rarely blinked.

By my twelfth birthday I had my own binoculars. I don't remember opening the present but I do remember later staring at the debris of floral wrapping paper around me, as though it were my cocoon too, and I'd just burst out into a new life. I'd seen all I wanted in the house and through its windows, and I started to take long walks, the binoculars strapped around my neck. My breasts, just beginning to grow, felt the weight bouncing against them as I climbed hills, trees, old abandoned buildings. From there new vistas were offered to me: the other sides of fences, the paint chipped and filthy; the bitter family arguments in the hidden, unkempt backyards. The binoculars taught me that anything, when seen from a different angle, lives again.

I instinctively applied this to the boys at school. During and between classes, whether shy or teasing, they were always afraid to hold anyone's eyes in their own. Yet when I watched the boys through the binoculars, practicing positions on the sports field, I saw them grow easier with themselves and each other. I realized that soon one of them would be that way with me, and we would eventually disappear into the same woods from which I was now watching.

This waiting kept me awake. Even late at night I was busy with my binoculars. I saw Father's dirty fingernails as he tried to quietly pour himself a drink in the soft light of the kitchen. Other nights I watched my mother in the study as she ransacked Father's desk for whatever it was she couldn't find. Once I followed my father into the backyard, and across the lawn I focused in on his unhappy, crying face and shaking shoulders. But what fascinated me most was his profile in the moonlight and how much of my own features I saw there, as though I were looking at myself through another's eyes.

I started opening my closet after school, poring over the dresses inside, examining the buttons, pleats, all the styles. I imagined myself dressed in each one and walking about as if I were in a crowd, pretending I wasn't being watched. Boys soon began to call. I was always late preparing. With the bedroom door open a crack I peered down past the banister to where the young man was contending with my parents. I surveyed every tick and twitch. I saw how his feet tapped in cross-rhythm to my mother's questions; I gaped at his easy shrug at my father's friendly, veiled threats. From this strong signature I predicted the pattern of the evening. While we walked in the dark to the car, our date, for me, was already over and I was quietly and excitedly reflecting upon it.

My parents eventually stopped speaking to each other and used me as a go-between. This didn't work out well— my interpretations of apparently meaningless gestures proved so accurate that my role was replaced by a dachs- hund. I left home shortly after high school graduation, though I had really been gone for years. I wrote postcards occasionally, and always separately, to my parents, and with them both I had little to say.

I worked as a secretary, and during lunch breaks I roamed the nearby park. That was where I first met my husband. He was walking along the edge of trees facing a field where a baseball game was in progress. He noticed me almost as soon as I had him in focus and waved to me. Holding the binoculars with one hand, I waved back. He sat down on one of the benches and motioned, very politely, for me to come and join him. I walked over, my hands around the lenses, my fingers playing with the leather straps that draped around my neck like a snug friend. When I sat down he asked me, politely, if I could make out from our bench the change-up signals passing between the catcher and pitcher. I said I wasn't sure—he interrupted and assured me he wasn't a member of the opposing team;

he was just curious. I explained that I didn't know anything about baseball. He said, "That's all right, you watch and I'll tell you what to look for."

From the beginning I came to know him by what he wanted to see and he came to know me by how I described it. That night, while in his still-warm car, I peered out and described the features of a distant, graceful statue in the park: the strong curve of the neck and slope of the shoulders, naked collarbone, and shadows circling the breasts. His hands curved over me, his lips closely following my careful, increasingly breathless descriptions until finally I dropped the binoculars. Later, when we took walks, I stared at the movement of his eyes, vainly hoping to anticipate what they would settle on. He would be over a stone fence before I could finish detailing the rough crystal surfaces, the interlocking patterns: instead I saw him beckoning to me from the field beyond. And I followed. But always I felt the pull of the lenses. How else could I see clearly the soft play of light on his face in the late afternoon or, while he napped, his barest flick of eyelash? During our wedding ceremony his eyes seemed to be locked on some point in the distance and I felt a great need to distinguish what it was, but I was lost without my binoculars. My agitation was apparent even to the guests, and it was the cause of the first bitter argument of our married life.

My husband grew less interested in distant patterns and my descriptions of them. I wanted to get out of the house, to discover new sights we could both hold in view, but he kept asking me to put away the binoculars. So I walked through the house, staring at everything, especially our wedding pictures on the bedroom bureau, though all I really wanted was to steal a glance at my husband, alone in his chair in the study. And each night I placed the binoculars in a new hiding place, half-hoping that the next day I would forget where I'd put them. Once, in the middle of the night, I rose and walked quietly to the living room and turned on the television, keeping the sound off. I stared at the silent images in the dark room. From up close the actors on the screen were transformed by the tiny electronic dots, and they played out passionate lives that I realized would continue no matter how carefully I stared, would continue even if the set was clicked off. So I made it all go blurry, my fingers turning the lenses farther and farther apart. Then I walked to a hall closet and placed the binoculars behind hats my husband never wore and I didn't return, no matter how often my fingers tingled.

When I became pregnant I watched the growth of my belly with curiosity, yet without the binoculars I couldn't focus on anything significant: only a lonely, dark hair, set apart from the light down of my skin; or my navel, somehow frightening the way it coiled inside itself like a secret ready to strike. Early one day, lying in bed, I surveyed the entire room from the horizon of my ascendant stomach. The shift in perspective, rather than intriguing, left me dizzy, my own form of morning sickness.

I was uncontrollable in the delivery room, my hands gripping an invisible pair of lenses. I received so much sedation that I recalled nothing of my daughter's birth and very little of my first viewings of her in the hospital. But when I returned home I stayed beside her for hours, gazing in fascination. I watched the random movement of her pink fingers like tiny flames in the breeze. I remembered how, as a child, I'd stare for hours at a pile of logs in the fireplace: I'd wonder how anything could let itself be consumed, and I'd watch from a distance as if it were contagious, though at the same time I would be drawn to it.

Through the Binoculars

Again I watched my child, her restless toes like hot little coals, and my fingers hovered over her, wanting to touch her warmth and yet afraid to touch it.

Now, with my husband away at work, I spend the days together with my daughter. I watch her fingers learn how to grasp and how to let go; I press her close to me, her soft hair tickling my hands; I whisper in her ears the beginnings of speech. But sometimes, just sometimes, I sit alone by a second-floor window and peer through my old binoculars. My daughter searches for me. She half-crawls, half-walks silently, instinctively, from room to room. She knows I'm sure to be in one of them, sitting with my back to the door, looking out through a window. When she sees me she begins to babble, little attempts at the words she's heard her father and me speak to her. I turn around and focus on the doorway: I watch her movements as she approaches. She smiles when she sees this; she thinks this is a game. But when she crawls closer I turn the binoculars around, and through them she seems so much smaller, so much farther away than she really is.

I Dreamt About You Last Night

Turley drove up the driveway in the semidarkness. His daughter, alone on the front lawn with her doll, ran toward him so quickly that he stopped the car abruptly. "Mommy's gone, Mommy's gone," she chanted, face contorted, and Turley stepped out and awkwardly picked her up. Her arms were cold. "Where is she?" he asked, but his daughter kept crying, her arms around his neck, her doll dangling down his back.

Turley unlocked the front door and they entered the house, but he stopped at the edge of the foyer. Inside, the walls were spray-painted with huge, dark words. WHAT? I CAN'T HEAR YOU sprawled above the couch, YES, I DID CALL THE DOCTOR hovered over the lamp in the corner: each sentence a lie he had once casually told his wife. These were small falsehoods, evasions she had never confronted him with before, he thought, yet he grew frightened at the angry catalog around him, frightened at what silence could do. He approached one stained wall, and his daughter leaned over from his embrace and touched the tip of a scrawled S.

"Why is the wall dirty?"

"It's nothing, Julie; they're just words."

I PROMISE IT WON'T HAPPEN AGAIN drew him down the hall, and when he looked into the bedroom doorway, he saw I DREAMT ABOUT YOU LAST NIGHT twisting above the bed. Turley walked throughout the house, remembering all the false moments of his marriage. His daughter grew restless in his arms and he put her down. She ran before him with her doll, pointing and calling back, "Look, Daddy, look!" He could see he would have to paint over every wall. But he was afraid that by then he would have memorized every word and they would follow him from room to room.

"Wooie," gasped the young man who came to paint.

"A party," Turley said. "It got a bit out of hand."

"Must have," said the young man, impressed, his ponytail swinging as he arranged his cans of paint. There were flecks of white in his hair. "What was the occasion?"

"I don't remember," Turley said, feeling stupid and naked. "It was a pretty wild party."

"Yeah, strange things can happen," the young man grunted as he carried in his drop cloths. "I was at a party once, people pulled up the rug—wall-to-wall carpeting—so everybody could dance."

Turley interrupted. "Would you like some coffee?"

"Nah, coffee's not good for you."

"I only have decaffeinated," he lied, softly, but the young man was already beginning to spread a thick cloth over the couch.

Turley stayed in the kitchen, feeling off-balance, stirring his coffee first with one hand, then with the other. Occasionally he could hear an *"Intense,"* or an "Oh, smokin'!" as the painter set up in a new room. Finally,

Turley walked quietly down the hall to inspect the work. He looked into the study, where the young man was carefully touching up the baseboard. On the wall the large words I NEVER TOUCHED YOUR LETTER were still faintly visible under the first coat of paint, an X-ray image.

He returned to the kitchen and shut all the half-open cabinet doors. He enjoyed the snap of closure, so he opened all the doors and closed them once again, two at a time, each hand evenly balanced on a handle. Turley thought of how, when all the dishes were dried and put away, his wife would say, "Let's play Domino." He'd give her a shove and she would run around the table as fast as she could, slamming all the open cabinet doors. He looked down at the messy counter. On the stove by a burner was the pepper shaker, a round ceramic face with a dark moustache. The salt shaker, its ceramic face a huge white smile, was on its side by the sink sprayer. Turley cleared a space on the counter, placed them together like a satisfied couple, and neatly arranged all the odd objects around them: a tattered bulb of garlic, a corkscrew, and three unpeeled, abandoned onions from some forgotten meal.

With everything in place, Turley walked slowly back to the table, taking care to arrive with an equal number of right and left footsteps. He sat and stirred his cold coffee: one turn of the spoon, his wife would phone; another turn, she wouldn't; a third turn, she'd walk in the front door; a fourth, she'd pass by the house and he'd never know. Slowly, as he stirred, without realizing it, Turley began to believe in magic.

In the mornings, Mrs. Hempill came to the house to take care of Julie. Turley didn't like her: she insisted on being paid daily. "Any word yet?" she always asked amiably, and Turley would look quickly, guiltily at a white wall.

"No, no word yet." It was as if his wife had vanished: no letter, no lawyer's demands over the phone. "Mommy's gone on a trip," he had told his daughter for days, but repeatedly he was lost in his inconsistencies and makeshift tales as she questioned him. "I don't know *when* Mommy's coming back!" he finally shouted, ashamed. Julie never asked again, and Turley was unsettled by this silence. Soon she became afraid of walking past open doors. "Something's hiding," she would say, and Turley had to keep all the doors in the house closed.

Turley sat on the couch at night in the freshly painted living room and remembered how his wife would put tracing paper over maps in the atlas and follow with a pencil the quickest route out of any city. He carefully tapped his fingers in time to each other, as if the world had invisible strings that only he could manipulate to draw his wife back home. Beside him his daughter pushed her dolls together into little dramas. "Give it *back*!" she said in a high-pitched voice as she held her bosomy female doll by the waist. "Give what back?" she replied in the lower voice of her formal-looking male doll as she made it face away. "You *know*. I *want* it!" she shouted and, guided by her hands, the two dolls threateningly circled each other. She looked at Turley. "Daddy, my dolls are being mean. Make them stop." But Turley sat staring as if they had come alive and led independent lives. Julie turned to her largest and favorite doll, sitting on a chair opposite them. Its grave, porcelain face with a faint smile seemed to listen as Julie quietly asked it for help in the same coaxing tones she used whenever she wanted something from her mother. But it remained silent, and she asked again in a louder, angry voice.

"Julie," Turley whispered, recovering, "your dolls are asleep," and he pointed to them lying on the rug. His daughter glanced down unhappily, knowing what was coming. "And it's your bedtime too," he added.

Turley tucked her in his arms and Julie held the three dolls as he carried her out of the living room. "Close the door," she reminded him, and he pulled it shut. In her bedroom Julie arranged the two smaller dolls on a shelf, but she wouldn't touch the largest. "I'm punishing her," she announced as she crawled into bed.

"Why?" Turley asked.

"Because I ask and ask but she won't talk to me."

"She'll talk to you someday," Turley said, immediately regretting this falsehood as he bent down to kiss his daughter.

"She will?"

"Shhh," he whispered, "go to sleep." On the wall above the bed his words A GIRL? THAT'S WONDERFUL! lay beneath the paint. He turned and closed the door behind him, knowing Julie was waiting to hear its click.

Turley went to bed early, happy for the walls to dissolve in darkness. He lay awake and stared at the ceiling. Once or twice a car drove by, and the passing light seeped through the blinds and raced across the walls.

He woke in the morning to Julie's crying. He ran to her bedroom and there on the floor was her favorite doll, torn and broken in pieces.

"She broke," Julie wailed, her palms pressed against her face.

"How?" Turley asked. He stepped around the doll's rubble and knelt beside his daughter. She peered at him through her fingers.

"She just broke."

He heard the lie in her voice as if it were his own, but he said nothing. He held her while she cried, her fingers clutching his shirt. When she calmed he dumped some crayons from an old shoe box and filled it instead with the parts of her doll.

He made breakfast. She sat silently while he cut her omelet into neat little squares. "I'll take your doll with me, okay? I'll have her fixed." Julie nodded yes and drank from her plastic cup, dripping orange juice onto the plate. When they were almost finished eating, Mrs. Hempill came to the front door. "Why so quiet?" she asked as Julie stared at her entrance. Turley and his daughter looked at each other conspiratorially. "She's still sleepy," he said. Mrs. Hempill turned to him. "Any word yet?" she asked cheerfully.

Though Turley knew there was nothing wrong with his car, as he drove to work, the shoe box beside him on the front seat, he kept imagining that at once, with no other traffic in sight, his engine would roar open a hole through the middle of the hood like a geyser. His body shuddered, and when he was finally downtown he parked the car with relief. He took an index card from his pocket and checked the address: the Doll Clinic was just a few blocks away. As he made his way down the crowded street, he scuffed one shoe and then the other for an opposite, sympathetic tingle. He remembered how when his wife was angry with him she would hold him close to dance and try to step on his feet. At the end of the block, waiting for the light to change, Turley carefully shifted the shoe box from under one arm to the other and thought of when he had once tossed his car keys from hand to hand, daring his wife to catch them if she really wanted to drive. As his secret rituals and memories converged, he looked for his wife among the people on the street across from him, but she wasn't there.

Inside the repair shop Turley was uncomfortable, surrounded as he was by the staring faces of rows of dolls. The woman at the register, her face heavily made up, was watching him as well, waiting for him to speak. Beside her on the counter was a doll whose dress, hinged like a door, was partly opened, revealing a scooped-out body lined with miniature pots, pans, and dishes.

"I need a doll repaired," Turley said nervously. He opened the shoe box.

"I'm sure we can . . ." the woman began, but paused when she saw the battered doll.

Turley spoke rapidly. "The dog got to it and ripped it up."

The woman took the doll from the box. Its dress was badly torn and at the ends of the limbs were the jagged remains of ceramic hands and feet. She examined the porcelain head, with its punched-in, loose left eye. "This may be a difficult job," the woman said. She pulled off the mohair wig, revealing the hollow skull of the doll, and she poked her fingers inside to manipulate the glass eye from behind. Turley found this almost impossible to watch.

"Strange," the woman said when she finally put down the doll, "these rips are unusual for teeth marks."

"It's an old dog," Turley said, and then he looked away from her to the morning traffic outside. "Its teeth are soft," he added, imagining these words spray-painted on his dining room wall. The woman's hands stroked the remains of the doll. "A shame. You must watch your dog more carefully. But don't worry, everything will be repaired."

Two nights later, while Turley was cleaning up after dinner and Julie was banging her dolls together by the sink, the phone rang. Before he answered, Turley decided it must be his wife. He imagined her at the other end of the line, holding the phone as she always did, the receiver nestled between chin and shoulder, one hand twisting the cord around the wrist of the other, as if strangling it. After the third ring he carefully lifted the receiver to his ear by slowly passing it from hand to hand, another secret ritual.

"Hello?"

"Hi, this is Jack . . . the painter."

"Oh," Turley said, confused and disappointed.

"Yeah, well, there's this party going on tonight, and since you seem to know a thing or two, I thought you might like to come along. My friends would like to meet you."

"Hey, thanks," Turley said, appalled, "but tonight's a bad night."

"Oh, got something going on over there?"

"Well . . ."

"No problem. I could even drop by later, I might learn something."

"Oh, no! Actually, I'll be out."

"I get it. That's cool. Catch you later."

"Yeah, sure," Turley replied. The receiver clicked. Julie was staring at him, and he felt the effort to twist his lips into a faint smile. "Hey," he said, "how about we go into the living room and play?"

Turley stood in the middle of the room. He was a mountain, and her dolls were trying to climb him, but they never made it to the top. As if his limbs could release like tumbling boulders, Turley shook and growled, "I'm an earthquake!" The dolls fell together to the floor, where they stalked each other, led by Julie's hands. Turley glanced over at the phone in the kitchen, hoping it would ring again, hoping it would be his wife. And what if she *did* call? he thought, remembering which of his lies had been painted near the kitchen doorway: IT'S OUR OWN LITTLE SECRET. Angry and miserable at his wife's pitiless revenge, Turley thought that he would tell his wife how happy he and Julie were, how they didn't need her. The dolls began to climb up his left arm. He shook and they fell. "I'm an earthquake!" he shouted.

The doll was repaired. It lay wrapped in tissue in its long white box on the front seat as Turley drove home. It had shiny new hands and feet—the fingernails delicate and painted pink, the shoes permanently polished—a left eye fully restored to the solemn face with the half-smile, and a frilled and flowered dress. When Turley entered his house, bending and kissing Julie, she carefully regarded his package. Mrs. Hempill began to put on her familiar smile, but Turley cut her off, saying, "No word yet." After she was out the door Turley opened the box with a grin and lifted the doll from the tissue.

"She's new," Julie said, reaching for it.

"Well, almost new," Turley replied, handing it to her, but she wasn't listening. She held the doll before her and stared at it quietly, her lips slightly turned up, as if she were in front of a mirror and the doll were her reflection.

"I fixed her," Turley said uneasily, frightened by this new lie, and he at once added, "I'll go make us some dinner."

In the kitchen, Turley concentrated on adjusting the heat for the rice, and reduced to a soft hiss the frying chicken breasts and carrots. He imagined that if each part of the meal finished cooking at the same time, he wouldn't tell another lie that night. Soon everything was equally simmering and ready.

While Turley served and cut Julie's portion, she settled her doll in the chair beside her. "She's hungry," Julie announced.

"Honey, dolls don't eat," Turley said as he went to the refrigerator for a beer.

"But you said you fixed her."

"I did," he affirmed nervously, returning, "but dolls don't like chicken." Once again his rituals had failed him, and he was afraid of what else he might say.

Julie put down her fork and looked at him, very interested. "What *do* they like?"

Turley glanced over at the chair where his wife used to sit and he hoped for her clear gaze and one of her canny interruptions. "They won't say," he finally replied. "They're very fussy."

Julie turned to her doll. "She'll tell *me*."

Turley remembered his old lie and said quickly, "She might not."

"But you said you fixed her."

"I *did*," he replied, raising his voice. "Now eat your dinner!"

They finished the meal in silence. Then Julie went back to the living room with her doll. Turley washed the dishes, aware that behind him on the wall lay buried the words I DIDN'T MEAN TO BREAK YOUR FAVORITE CUP. When he finally came in and joined her, Julie got up and walked to the other side of the room, whispering to her doll. Turley feigned indifference and turned on the television. When it was time for her bed, she didn't argue, and he picked up his daughter and the doll and carried them down the hall.

In bed, Julie's fingers played with the ends of her blanket and she looked over at her doll across the room in a small rocking chair. "Good night," Turley whispered, kissing her, and he turned off the light and left softly. He moved away from the door after closing it so Julie couldn't see the shadows from his feet, and he stepped evenly in place, loudly, then softly, as if he were walking down the hall. Then he waited.

Through the closed door Turley heard first his daughter rise from bed, then her bare feet on the floor. He was sure she was coming toward him, but before he could run down the lighted hall, he heard Julie say, "I know you can talk." Then she said, "I missed you. Did you miss me?" Her doll didn't reply. "Do you want to play?" Julie asked and, again, silence. "It's just us. *Talk*."

Turley stood in the hallway, suppressing a cough, aware of every subtle itch he was afraid to scratch, and he listened to Julie continue her pleading. "You're prettier than ever," she repeated again and again. Turley closed his eyes, and he could see his daughter, lonely in her room before the dark figure of the doll, trying to invoke the impossible, impatient at her inability to induce a quiet confidence. Julie began to threaten. "When I wake up, you *better* talk."

Turley heard his daughter pad back to bed. He remained still and listened to her occasional rustlings under the blanket. He felt exposed under the glare of the hall light, and he imagined that his wife was somehow about to appear and loudly discover him. He slowly, silently counted the seconds to repel her memory, to record a reasonable time before he dared move and make a sound, knowing that on the wall across from him I WASN'T SNOOPING lay beneath the paint.

When Julie's room was finally quiet, instead of tiptoeing away Turley opened the door and walked to her bedside. Julie's lips were softly trembling silent words in her sleep, just as his wife had often done. He looked at her closely. Where did his wife stop in his child's face and where did he begin, and whose lips whispered what words from what dream? Turley turned to leave, and as he passed the doomed doll in the tiny rocking chair he wondered how its broken body would look in the morning. Its steady gaze frightened him, and he clicked the door closed.

He was exhausted and felt ensnared in his accumulating falsehoods. He switched off the television, the lights, and walked to the bathroom, where he turned on the water from the shower head and adjusted the temperature. His left foot tingling, still half-asleep from standing, Turley undressed in front of the mirror and was suddenly afraid of what he saw. Under the harsh fluorescent light he could see the symmetrical trails of blue veins that traveled his pale body, half of his blood running to his heart, the other half running away. He turned off the light, felt his way to the tub, and showered in the dark.

He dried himself quickly and then walked carefully to bed, his hand sweeping before him in the darkness. In bed, he slowly turned under the covers, and when he lay still he could feel the force of his monotonous, trembling heart as he thought of all the lies on the walls. When he was finally asleep, Turley dreamt that his bones began to grow fluorescent in his body, beginning with his jaw and spreading down the spine and limbs until they gleamed against his frail and hidden muscles and organs. When he lifted his hands the bones glowed, illuminating a mirror on the wall. He walked to it and stared, terrified, at his livid skull, at the shining sockets beneath the gristle of his nose, and he ran from this vision. But as he rushed through the rooms the walls flared bright, his own dark words now visible through the paint and surrounding him. He continued to tear through the house, his feet aching, his lungs beating against the blaze of his ribs, and he tried to leave his glowing body behind, but how could he escape from his own terrible light?

Shadows

Something was missing: I'd struggled with this portrait for days, this portrait of a woman I tried to imagine, and still there was something my carefully drawn lines couldn't manage to contain. The nose was still only a faint outline, the one large eye had no twin to stare with, and each uncertain curve of hair had been erased until I was afraid to try again. Yet when I decided to tear off the sheet from the pad, the shadow of my hand seemed to continue where the pencil had left off, trying to fill the blanks I had left, as though wanting to leave part of itself on the page. Frightened, I raised my hand away from the drawing. My shadow faithfully followed, making me unsure of what I had seen, and for the rest of the evening it reflected every movement I made, no matter how complex. Nevertheless, I was uncertain whether this was obedience or skillful plagiarism.

The next few days I felt myself being followed by a dark, fun-house mirror that distorted, just slightly, every step I took, every gesture I made. It seemed to cast its arm impatiently through the sleeve before my own when I put on a shirt, and then it walked bowlegged behind me. Whenever I took up the unfinished portrait, as I idly tapped my fingers I noticed my shadow was out of rhythm. When I stared it moved back into place, but each time taking longer to return.

At night I was afraid that the shadow, in its element, was tracing patterns and growing in power. And indeed, it finally threw off the sham of mimic and began to take over. One night I dreamt I was a collapsing star, unable to cast any light. I awoke in darkness and, restless, I stretched for the lamp: I kept twisting its knob but nothing happened. My eyes then slowly focused on the bulb and the shadowy hand that was wrapped around the intermittent faint glow, keeping the room in darkness. It was then clear to me that we no longer led parallel lives.

In the morning, the shadow easily shed me and seeped down the stairs, the unfolding of an ominous welcoming carpet. It stood at the front door, waiting as I descended, its hand held in a gesture of *After you.*

"No," I whispered.

Who could have predicted such rage? It threw itself against the door, the walls, finally me. I was covered with blows I couldn't feel, yet I hurt inside as if something had been wrenched loose. When the shadow calmed down, hunched like a black ball in the corner, I realized I couldn't cast anything of myself against the wall. There was no dark twin to greet my hand when it approached a surface, nothing of myself to meet me each careful, untethered step I took throughout the house. I stopped at the doorway of my small study, where the shadow was waiting for me, sitting by my drawing pad at the table and attempting to pick up a pencil with its fingers again and again. It turned up its dark, featureless face as I entered the room, and it cradled the pad as if to say, *Here, you try.*

For days I remained inside, possessed by the sight of other shadows. I watched the slender, dark legs of chairs stretched across the floor; the black twin of the wall clock's minute hand, keeping its own time; and the graceful shadows of the lightly swaying trees outside my window. Throughout, I envied my own: its lack of fatigue and hunger, its shedding of pain, smell, me. It sat close by in a quiet rage, unable to move the pencil, unable to employ my aid, able only to mime pencillike movements. In frustration it turned to caricature and parody. Cramped for hours in another shadow, it waited until I unknowingly glanced its way. Then, the shadow of the unoccupied rocking chair began to rock. Dark images of books fell from the shelves and without thinking I ran to grab them. The spider plant's shadow grew out of shape and intricately stained the walls. Even though I knew what was behind all of this, I felt as if every shadow in the house would soon dangerously release itself.

I decided it was time to leave, alone. I stood by the plant stand next to the door, pretending to examine the leaves of a fern for dry rot, hoping to give no clues to my real intention. I waited until the shadow was deeply engrossed in the sketch pad, and I slipped out. But as soon as I shut the door, it was beside me. Immediately it began to outpace me, threatening to leave me in its wake. Each stride *I* was forced to match it, not the other way around. We were hurrying down a crowded street where it was difficult to distinguish my shadow from others, much less keep up with the dark beast. I could have easily fallen behind and slipped down an alley, yet I had somehow turned from hunted to hunter. Then, without warning, the shadow rushed across the street and I followed close behind, but I soon forgot the chase. Approaching from the other direction was a woman with a look of desperation in her oddly familiar face: she too was walking just a bit too fast, with her steps just a bit shy of *her* shadow's. She noticed me, and we slowed, then stopped and stared at our shared plight. Our shadows also stopped and stared at each other. All four of us were filled with an incredible longing.

The Art of the Knock

We began to—how can I put it?—*double-date*. Yet she and I only pretended to be comfortable with our companions as we sat on a park bench, and we whispered about our recent troubles with our shadows and their obsessions with portraits that both of us had been unable to complete, portraits that—could it be?—vaguely reminded us of each other. We held hands, amazed at the easy, complementary fit of fingers, we leaned close together and hesitantly kissed, and out of the corners of our eyes we carefully watched our shadows on the meadow in their own clinch.

We sat there for a long time, afraid of disturbing the shadows. When we finally stood as if to leave, they simply complied and followed. Yet was this only because, as we passed by the lake, they could shimmer joyfully together? When we reached my home the shadows, larger than we, loomed over the front door and blended in with its dark grain. They seemed to be a part of it, waiting to be opened. We slowly entered and embraced nervously, and from the bright light in the hall our shadows rose together above us. We stopped kissing. Surprised, they stopped too. Then, in amused silence, we all turned back to each other.

Now, in the evenings, my love and I collaborate: her watercolors with my graphics. When her bright washes spread past my carefully etched lines, oozing energy, or when I draw in details at odds with the mood of her colors, the contrasts of our work seem to unite us even more, even as our shadows pass across the page while we compose.

And at night, after lovemaking, after we pull up the twisted sheets and settle in the dark, we notice that the bed is still insistently shaking: and we let their passion rock us to sleep.

Falling Stars

Sylvie woke to the sound of her husband's fingers tapping against the mattress. Her ears filled with the reverberations. Lying on her side, she opened her eyes to see the back of his head and wispy, ruffled hair. He was lying on his stomach, and his hands were under the pillow, where they continued to tap nervously. "Jeff?" Sylvie whispered. "What's the matter, honey?" But Jeff kept twitching his fingers, and Sylvie hadn't expected him to answer. This wasn't the first time recently that he had ignored her, and she was beginning to fear that it was far from the last. Sylvie pinched the small roll of flesh on her stomach. She could diet again, but she knew that after all her suffering to lose a pound, he wouldn't notice and she'd end up gaining two. Well, *let* him pretend he can't hear me, she thought.

She rose out of bed and, on her way to the bathroom, she looked down at her husband. He seemed to have fallen from a great height, and the rumpled sheets he lay on were the curves of earth that now fit his body. Sylvie imagined he must have jumped from a lover's balcony: those restless fingers were probably all that his last bits of brain could manage, and he'd die knowing that he couldn't pull his pants back up from around his ankles. Serves you right, Sylvie thought as she squeezed too much toothpaste out of the tube, for sniffing after that Rhonda Davis. Sylvie gazed at her round face and sucked in her cheeks, thinking of how she might look once again if she lost a little weight.

As Jeff lay on the bed, the sound of running water in the bathroom sounded like the distant drone of a rescue plane. *SOS,* he continued to tap out, *SOS*—the only Morse code he could remember from an old war movie. His fingers faked a further message: *Hair falling out, please send help.* The water stopped and his wife began to brush her teeth. Jeff opened one eye and looked across the mattress before him for any stray hairs. There were none. But this was no comfort because he knew the latest deserters would be on the pillow. Traitors, he thought. Jeff lay there quiet and miserable as his wife walked from the bathroom, dressed, and left. It was Saturday and the boys were still asleep, but he knew she'd start breakfast anyway. Jeff sat up. The mirror was waiting for him, and it had no mercy. It was just a huge, damn eye and it saw everything. Jeff walked straight toward it, for it would not be disobeyed.

He patted his hair to the left, to the right, and forward down to his eyes, but always his scalp peeked through. If I were blond, you wouldn't notice so much, Jeff thought, and he briefly considered dyeing his hair. But that would probably cause more to fall out. He closed his eyes and tried to remember his thick and wavy hair. In his imagination his wife, younger and still slim, stood beside him. Though she was gaining too much weight, he didn't know just what to say to her. Jeff patted his own spreading stomach. He looked down at the strands in the sink, and then back at his forehead. *"Stay,"* he threatened his hair, as if it were some disobedient dog. "Stay," he repeated, over and over, coaxingly, unsure of his authority.

"What's Bruiser doing in the bathroom?" he heard his wife ask from the hall.

The bathroom door closed in Sylvie's face, and again Jeff didn't answer. She was angry, but she had to get back to her pancakes. "If you're washing Bruiser in there, make sure he doesn't get his paws on my rag rug!" she shouted. Sylvie returned to the kitchen, where Bruiser was at the screen door, having heard his name called out, and he barked his hungry bark. What is the *matter* with that man? she thought, surprised, as she let in the dog.

The television came on in the living room, with the sound of bombs and bullets and dying cartoon characters. "Willy," she called out, "fix Bruiser his food." Her son ran into the kitchen and opened the cupboard door. He held the can to his chest and twisted his mouth. "Joey," he whined to his older brother, "I'm gonna get more pancakes 'cause *I'm* helping Mom."

"Hush," Sylvie said, "you'll both get as much as you want."

When Sylvie fed her sons they ate silently. Their father was late for breakfast and Sylvie angrily flipped the pancakes on their plates. She turned to look at Jeff when he finally walked in. He wasn't wearing his glasses.

"You can't see," she said.

"Can too," Jeff replied, "and I'm not hungry." He walked out into the yard and Bruiser followed.

Who are *you* trying to lose weight for? Sylvie thought. She sat down with the boys, considered *her* extra pounds, and ate Jeff's portion as well as her own. Then, while Willy and Joey washed the dishes and argued, she began to bake. Today was the old Mooler twins' birthday, and there was going to be a big party in the afternoon. Sylvie gathered her eggs and flour and sugar together, and she heard Jeff outside begin to mow the lawn. So *that's* why he's got his glasses off, she thought while cracking eggs. Soon that Rhonda Davis will wander down the road like she did last week and he'll stop and talk. And squint too, she almost laughed to herself. Sylvie let the sugar sift through her fingers on its way to the bowl. She imagined she was at a beach far away, where all the little particles of sand were sweet. While the waves refined them to sugar she would let the sun tan her crisp on the vast, white, delicious shore.

Jeff could barely see where he was going with the lawn mower, but he didn't care: without his glasses, his hair appeared fuzzy, thicker. It didn't matter that there was no mirror before him, because he carried an invisible one inside him and it was satisfied, even if the breeze was careless with his combed hair. He saw himself as a captain in a storm and his hair was abandoning ship. The lawn mower shot the shredded grass into the air like sprays of parting waves, and the skitter of the sharpened blades sounded like the nervous flapping of wind in the sails. At the prow of his mower, Jeff steered an unsteady path through his backyard. His eyesight was worse than he remembered: he was truly falling apart. What else was about to begin its slow drift to oblivion? Jeff was about to list silently an inventory of parts when he slammed the mower blades into the yellow jackets' nest at the edge of his property. Soon he was circling his arms wildly about him, as though he were drowning and the bees were the splashing water. Jeff ran, and though the house was a blur before him, he headed straight for the kitchen door.

Sylvie's hands were full of cake mix when she heard Jeff shouting. She looked out the window: the sky was dark behind him with bees. She rushed to the sink to wash her hands as Jeff sped into the kitchen and slammed the screen door shut, leaving the angry, buzzing cloud outside. But a few had flown in with Jeff and he ineffectually swatted away at them as he hopped from the refrigerator to the sink to the kitchen table. "Help, help!" he howled. Their two round-faced boys stared through an open slit of door. "Shut that and stay *out,*" Sylvie shouted, and it shut. She grabbed a *People* magazine from the counter, folded it in half, and started swinging at the bees around Jeff's head. But she mostly missed and instead hit Jeff on the forehead and along the side of his face. She was hitting his bee stings and he hooted from the pain. But it felt good to Sylvie. Take *that* for rutting after Rhonda, she thought, and she smacked his ear. Jeff screamed. Sylvie grew graceful in her rage, dancing around her husband and slapping her magazine against every red welt she could see, only pretending to swat at the bees. Then she nicked one and it dove toward her. This is serious, she thought, and she ducked, opened the kitchen cabinet and grabbed the Raid. She and Jeff soon were coughing and waving their arms at nothing in the air, and the bees lay twisting on the kitchen floor.

Sylvie looked over at her bowl of cake batter. Uncovered and exposed to the settling poison, it was ruined. She turned and grabbed the *People* and slapped Jeff hard against his head. "There was a bee crawling on your shoulder," she said to his confused and wary gaze, and she pointed to one of the dead bees on the floor. "See? I got him."

"Jeez, hon, you're a pretty bad shot with that magazine," Jeff said. *Hon,* he had the nerve to call her. "If you'd just stayed still, I'd've had a better chance," she said, trying to hide the anger in her voice.

Jeff delicately patted his forehead: his face was already beginning to puff out. He was almost unrecognizable as

Jeff, and this helped Sylvie forget what a terrible husband he was, and she began to feel sorry for him. "Sit down," she said gently. He did, his half-closed eyes staring forward. "Willy! Joseph!" Sylvie called to their two sons, still hiding behind the closed door. "Bring some rubbing alcohol and cotton balls from the bathroom!"

"C'mere," she said to the puffy face, "let's get you on the couch." She led her husband to the living room and settled him just as Joey ran down the stairs, arms full, with Willy crying behind him. "He wouldn't let me carry *anything*," he whined.

"You two *behave*," Sylvie said. She had Willy hand her a cotton ball, had Joey lightly dab it with rubbing alcohol, and then applied the soggy thing to her husband's face.

"Is Dad gonna be okay?" Willy asked.

"Sure, he's chipper already," Sylvie said nervously, as Jeff squirmed on the couch from the pain.

She covered his face with rubbing alcohol until she was dizzy from the smell. She stood up and leaned on the arm of the couch for balance. "Let's give your father some rest," she said. She looked down at Jeff. He was a mess, but he was lying quietly and so Sylvie walked softly back to the kitchen to start her cake again from scratch.

The pain in Jeff's face felt like layers of fallen rock. He was buried alive: his nostrils were distant airholes, his field of vision was reduced to a pinpoint, and the sound of his family in the kitchen seemed miles away. Where did I go wrong? he thought. How could I have hit that hive? Jeff tried not to think about the attack of bees. Instead, he called up small moments of the morning: his wife's questioning voice, her blurred, frowning face as he had passed her on his way outside. He felt bad about snubbing breakfast, but he'd been angry with Sylvie for catching him talking to his hair in the bathroom. Then Jeff instantly worried: what do bee stings do to hair? His whole head burned; his hair must be a forest razed by fire. He heard Sylvie opening cupboards and shifting bowls around on the counter. She was *cooking* again; couldn't she ever stop? No wonder she'd kept missing the bees, hitting him instead, Jeff thought angrily, all that extra weight made her clumsy. Willy and Joey began to argue in the kitchen over who would break the eggs. Jeff lifted his hand up to his hairline and wished that his sons could somehow get along.

By the time Sylvie's cake was finished, its chocolate icing sculpted and shining in the afternoon light, she was already a little late for the Moolers' birthday party. Her boys had gone ahead of her. She looked in on Jeff. His swelling had subsided a bit and he looked more like her unfaithful husband. "Jeff? I'm going to the party now. When I come back I'll fix you something to eat." No answer. He was either asleep or ignoring her again. Sylvie picked up her cake, let Bruiser in so he wouldn't follow, and began the quarter-mile walk to the Moolers'.

Sylvie had gone about four blocks when she heard skidding tires and then a muffled crash around the corner ahead of her. She walked quickly toward the commotion, carefully balancing her cake. When Sylvie turned down the side street she saw the nose of Tom Dundee's old Buick buried in his front yard's neatly trimmed hedge. Betty Dundee was running out of their white frame house.

"Dammit, dammit, dammit!" Betty screamed, a giant-size bottle of cola in her fat hand. Tom flopped out of the car, drunk and unhurt, and he lurched away from his wife and tried to hide behind a shrub. Betty shook the cola bottle and squirted it at Tom. His front shirt sopping, he jumped into his wife's flower bed, where he knew she wouldn't follow. She hopped from one large foot to the other, taking swipes at Tom's head with the now-empty plastic bottle. Neighbors were gathering around the Dundees' property, and having an audience seemed to make Betty even angrier. She began to scream out unspeakable things, and Tom started crying. Then Betty started up too, and that was when Sylvie turned and walked off, appalled. She saw that she'd pressed her fingers into the side of the cake and now her nails were smeared with icing. She was suddenly ashamed of her earlier anger at Jeff.

Though Sylvie arrived late at the Moolers', the party was just starting. The breads hadn't been touched yet, not even the loaves in the shapes of airplanes and baseball mitts. As Sylvie put down her cake, she looked at the doughy gloves with satisfied surprise: someone had put an apple in the palm of each one. *Everything* was lovely, she thought. On the center of each card table was an Appetizer Tree, with tasty morsels stuck to the tips of the colorful plastic branches. "Eat up, everybody," said Jack Mooler, grandson to the twins. Sylvie quickly moved from one plastic tree filled with squares of American cheese to another almost stripped already of its cocktail wieners. She picked one of the last from a bottom branch. There were mustard stains on the tablecloth, but no bowl of mustard. Two Mooler great-grandchildren ran past the table. "Watch out, watch out!" shouted Rhonda Davis from behind Sylvie. "Those branches are sharp and they'll puncture your eyes!" Sylvie turned and looked at her. Rhonda was not only too thin and wore too much eye makeup, she had an evil temper. It was probably too much to hope that she'd choke to death on something during the party.

Sylvie walked off to the Moolers' back porch to search for mustard. She found a bowl on a table with a row of glasses filled with beer. The mustard was hotter than she'd expected and so she grabbed a glass and took cold sips right down to the bottom. She scanned the crowd for her two boys. They were waiting their turn at the swings and their faces were dirty with food. Buddy Mullen, standing alone by the driveway, saw Sylvie's searching face and he walked toward her with an easy swagger. His mouth, as always, was strained at the corners, as though he were holding back a laugh. But whenever Sylvie talked with him he had something sad to say: someone had sliced off a tip of finger while carving a roast; a mysterious fire had burned down an ailing business; an awful thing had crawled out of a piece of fruit his wife had bought at the produce market. Sylvie had always been a bit nervous around Buddy, but now she disliked him as she saw him approach: she could imagine how his face would look as he told someone about Jeff's bee stings. She didn't want to hear what Buddy had to report, and so she decided to spend a few minutes in the bathroom. Inside, Nancy Mooler, one of the twins' daughters, pointed her down a hallway.

Sylvie heard a rustling in the living room as she passed, and she peeked in through the almost closed door. The room was already a bit darkened from the late afternoon sky, yet she could make out Rhonda sitting by herself on the couch, impatient. Well, Sylvie thought, my Jeff isn't coming, so you can sit by yourself *all night*. Then Marvin Tisdale, whose wife was always away visiting her sick mother, appeared from a corner of the room and sat down beside Rhonda. He put his hand on her breast and whistled the "You deserve a break today" jingle. Rhonda laughed and grabbed Marvin's hand and led it lower. Sylvie quietly padded off to the bathroom. So, Rhonda was having an affair with Marvin, not Jeff. Or maybe she was just cheating on Jeff because he wasn't at the party. Imagine, Sylvie thought indignantly as she poked around curiously in the medicine cabinet, that Rhonda cheating on *my* husband!

When Sylvie walked back out on the porch a crowd was gathering around Jack Mooler. "All right, all right!" he shouted. "It's time for the grannies to open their presents!" Liz and Tess Mooler, those dedicated twins, were eighty years old today. They had married the Mooler brothers years ago so they could continue to have the same last name. They'd long since outlived their husbands and now were surrounded by friends, neighbors, and generations of Moolers. As they stood before the card table covered with brightly wrapped gifts their tears ran down identical wrinkles. Sylvie sat and watched from a distance as the twins opened presents that would probably last longer than they would. "Matching mugs," Liz said, and Tess held them up and slowly turned in a circle. "A melon scooper," Tess said, and Liz held it up and turned in a circle. By the time they were done it was almost dark. Sylvie called her boys over to her and sent them home. "I'll be right along," she said. But she stayed in her chair and drank down the line of beer glasses, only nibbling food here and there. While the stars came out Sylvie wished Jeff were with her; she wished they were drinking together.

Jeff awoke in a darkened room to the sound of his sons arguing. Each accusation and whine actually hurt him. "Shut *up!*" he shouted, and when his face seemed to explode he realized the pain was from his bee stings. The boys walked in silently. "You all right, Dad?" Joey asked. As quietly as he could, trying to barely move his lips, Jeff asked, "Where is your mother?" He listened carefully and when he just lay there, not saying anything, Willy and Joey left the room.

Jeff lay still for a long time. Slowly, he began to realize

he was famished, as the pangs of his stomach began to rival the pain of his aching face. Where *was* Sylvie, and what was taking her so long to return? She was probably still stuffing her face at that damn party. Jeff decided to fetch her, though his whole face felt swollen. His glasses seemed to press against his temples. He sneaked out carefully, not wanting the boys to hear and pester him to come along. As he walked outside, every footstep shuddered up to his head memories of his unfortunate morning. His head, he thought, must be cratered from bee impacts, and he could visualize his hair as dead stumps lying across a ravaged landscape. He grew more and more furious with his wife for making him come after her in his condition, overpowering any relief he might feel when he finally found her. I won't say anything when I find her, he thought; she'll have to beg and scream before I'll say even one little word. Soon he was approaching the field and small patch of woods just before the Moolers', and his anger rolled before him like a red carpet. He was even ready to slap her for eating all evening long while he had suffered alone, hurt, and hungry.

There was almost no one else at the party when Sylvie finally left, taking one awkward, drunken step after another under the beautiful, clear sky, a perfect night for forgiveness. I've been wrong about Jeff and evil to him, Sylvie thought as she weaved and hiccupped along the road to the woods, I'll be good, I'll try to be better. The path darkened as she entered the woods and she tried to walk, slowly and carefully, as straight as the line of glasses she'd drunk. When she came out into the field Sylvie stopped, dizzy, and stared at the black sky. A star fell, a swift white streak, followed by another and then another. Was the whole world coming to an end? she thought briefly in her guilt, confused. Then a star passed blazing a few inches from her face, and she realized she was surrounded by fireflies. Sylvie stood still, amazed at the display, and then she saw Jeff walking slowly down the road toward her. My husband has come for me, she thought; he *does* care. She watched Jeff's silent, deliberate approach. The fireflies *were* stars, she was sure as she stood unsteadily, surrounded by their lights, and suddenly the whole vast sky shrank to her small corner of light. She felt she was in the center of space, the still point of all there was, and the heavens circled and flared all around her.

Ancient Music

That night Mr. and Mrs. Michaels cheated at Scrabble. He asked for a glass of water, and when she left the room he flipped through the dictionary, looking for words beginning with the letter *z*. In the kitchen, Mrs. Michaels could hear the pages turning, and when she came back he was counting up his fifty-eight points for *zooid*. "What's that?" she asked, thinking to trap him. But he peered at her as if she were far away, her ignorance barely bridgeable. "Any organism capable of a separate existence, of course," he said. Mrs. Michaels kept quiet. She didn't even complain when all she could manage was surrounding a vowel already on the board with her only consonants, for *rat*. "What's the score?" she asked, and while Mr. Michaels touched the tip of his pencil to the numbered columns, she quickly palmed two of her four *a*'s and returned them to the box where she chose her new letters. Mr. Michaels heard more clicks and scrapes than there should have been, but he kept his head lowered until his wife was done, when he announced, "You're still ahead." But at the end of the game their scores were tied, the first time they could ever remember this happening. Each filled with guilty knowledge, they were both grateful neither of them had won.

"Well, Mr. Michaels," she said, this formal name having long ago transformed into tenderness, "I think that's enough for one night, don't you?"

"Yes, I suppose," he replied, but she was already walking up the stairs, leaving the lights for him. He checked the rooms on the first floor, leaving the kitchen for last. He pressed the refrigerator door to make sure it was closed and then he looked out the window at the backyard. He could see in the porch light the yellow-green buds of the trees hovering tentatively, feeling the pull of the branch and the pull of the wind as well. He flicked off the light switch and slowly walked up to the bedroom.

Mrs. Michaels heard her husband's careful footsteps. Standing naked in the lamplight, weary of her body, she quickly pulled her nightgown over her head. When he opened the bedroom door she glanced at him as if she were hiding a secret behind her back. He didn't notice and rolled up one of her sleeves and tickled her elbow. "This is where all your pretty wrinkles began, Mrs. Michaels, all those years of leaning on the table," he said, and then kissed it, forgiving her this irrevocable mistake.

"You were always wrinkled," she whispered in his ear, "I can't remember a time when you weren't," and at this fib he led her down to the bed where they slowly twisted the blankets beneath them. His hands against her back called up for her a darkened room forty years ago when the blinds, lit by the lamp outside, had swayed as they both had on the bed. Her knees rocking against his echoed for him an ancient summer, when they had floated on a raft so far from shore no one could have seen what they were doing. But their eyes always opened to the present, to each other's aged faces. Soon she felt a warm release, a small reminder of distant, stronger evenings. Her thin breasts brushing against the sheets, she remembered a greeting card he had sent her long ago, how its pale, printed flowers had only hinted at his darker passion. "Oh, Mr. Michaels," she cried, "oh, Mr. Michaels!"

Later, she listened to him breathing quietly beside her, the room around them absolutely black, and she imagined she was lying in a field. Above her, clouds shaped like words passed by—a long white list of first names. Her husband's was somewhere among them and she waited for its approach, though the sky grew darker and she fell asleep.

When Mr. Michaels died in the early morning, he floated up through the bedsheets to the ceiling, then slowly into the attic, the old suitcases and rolled-up rugs barely visible in the dark. Finally his eyes breached the roof and the shingles receded as he quickly drifted up in the air. But the long view of the surrounding town and the distant horizon, the sun still hidden, made him dizzy. There wasn't any place he wanted to be but home, so he imagined his feet were weighted, each toe fat, each foot heavy. He slowly fell and thought of where he wanted his feet to take him: to the kitchen for the breakfast smell of butter melting into toast, then to the living room to feel the serrated edges of the rare domestic issues of his stamp collection. As he thought of the thick lenses of his glasses on the night table, his feet slipped through the bedroom ceiling, his entire form descending in the air to the carpeted floor. There he stared at his still body and waited for his wife to wake up. It wasn't until she opened her eyes that he realized what she saw—his quiet figure, its absence of breath easily discovered as she placed her palm against his nostrils. Then she slowly moved her hand down to his chest and held it there for a very long time, her face pressed against his shoulders. Only when she sat up could he see her smeared and silent tears.

Mrs. Michaels closed her eyes. She didn't want to see the room or anything in it. She groped for the door to the hallway, and even if her eyes had been open she wouldn't have seen her husband, hovering and arms wide to embrace her, as she passed through him. At the stairs she stopped and looked down at the light slanting through the living room curtains. "This is an ordinary day," she said aloud. "The sun is up. Nothing has happened." But when she looked back past the bedroom doorway, her husband's motionless figure silently refuted her.

His body was soon carried from the house by strangers and driven off. Mr. Michaels stood by the window, the sunlight passing through him as he watched the vanishing car. He waved good-bye and his hand passed through the glass pane, near where a fly was resting. He pulled his hand back inside and trapped it, easily. But the fly continued rubbing its thin legs together, unaware of his enveloping, invisible hand. It flew through his fingers to a lampshade. He followed and captured it and again it escaped in contented and unpredictable flight. While he chased the fly about the house with an anger and frustration that almost convinced him he was alive, his wife remained upstairs, silent before the unmade bed.

The phone rang through the day, interrupted by Mrs. Michaels' long and sad conversations. The children began to arrive—the only son, the three daughters. Unseen, Mr. Michaels examined them closely. They looked old, and he felt that he was a child and they were his parents. He couldn't bear this, but when he closed his eyes he saw right through his transparent lids. He quickly glided away to the laundry room—the quietest part of the house—and slid through the curved metal door of the hamper and hid. He settled among the soiled clothes and listened to the murmur of familiar voices that pulled at him like fingers. When the house was empty, the family far away at his wake and then funeral, he came out to practice his new existence and he sat for hours in the wing chair, balancing his elbows so they wouldn't sink down into the upholstered arms.

After the funeral everyone returned to the house for a farewell lunch. The large families of his children crowded the rooms and mingled with the neighbors and friends. No one was aware of him. He listened but soon grew depressed because he couldn't recognize himself in their stories. He didn't remember any roller-coaster ride or repairing a bicycle. He wandered off and found himself following his great-grandchildren—two boys—who were walking uncertainly away from the adults. He stared at their strange, tiny faces, but he still couldn't recall their names. They babbled in an almost-English that they seemed to understand as they circled each other. One tottered and, off-balance, grabbed at the other and they both fell. Mr. Michaels fell too, in sympathy, but at their cries the boys were swept up by their mothers and he sat alone. He stayed there and watched his wife. She insisted on organizing everything—the sandwiches, the passing of cold beer, the requests for coffee. Only when she paused did he see the frantic look in her eyes. He returned to the hamper and stared for hours at a sock curled in on itself.

Mrs. Michaels overlooked the slow departure of friends and family. Sally, her oldest daughter, offered to stay a few days but was thanked and refused. Sally herself was a grandmother and she looked so old Mrs. Michaels couldn't wait for her to leave. When she was finally alone she closed the curtains to hide her own reflection. Then she walked to the laundry room. She stood before the hamper and opened it. Out spilled the clothes and her husband, though she didn't see his confused, invisible tumbling. Instead, she separated his clothes from hers, determined not to wash them and erase his smell, his stains. She carried them to the bedroom and hung his shirts and pants in the closet, folded and settled his underwear and socks in the dresser. When she closed the doors, she felt that somehow she was holding him inside.

Mr. Michaels quickly discovered death has no sleep, and day and night became for him a turning of light and dark. At night, while his wife slept alone, he sat awake in a chair downstairs. He missed dreams and invented his own from the sounds outside. When he heard the hiss of a car passing in the street he became its driver, chased by something swift and unseen. In the summer heat the moths tapping against the windows were the footsteps of someone whose arrival he constantly awaited. During the day he wandered in the house, trying to avoid his wife, for though he was the ghost, her sorrow was haunting *him*. She read paragraphs aloud from the newspaper and then stopped, embarrassed at the sight of his empty chair. All the while he was pacing across the room, but he had long given up responding. At these moments he felt a tug at his shoulders, as if he were connected to strings. He realized he belonged somewhere else and he had only to let himself float up and he would find it, but something always held him back.

One evening Mrs. Michaels set the table for two as she prepared dinner—minute steaks, rice boiled in chicken broth, buttered broccoli. But no one arrived for the meal by the time she filled the plates and sat alone to eat. Mr. Michaels hesitated at first, then he sat down at his place.

He pretended he could lift a knife and fork and picked at his untouched portions. Beyond hunger, he watched her. A pressure to rise pulled at his shoulders. It's time to leave, he thought, and his feet rose.

Mrs. Michaels' sorrow suddenly seized her and she pushed back from the table and leapt up. She quickly left the kitchen and searched in the rooms for her dead husband, as if it were all a trick and he were only hiding. She peered into the closets, the hangers screeching against the metal poles as she pushed them aside. She bent down to stare at the cool dark under the beds. She didn't know he was behind her, drawn by her search, his shoulders no longer tingling. He hoped he *could* be found, that somehow they both would find him in a corner with dust on his fingers, and a slight smile on his ashamed face. But finally, in the basement, coming out from a pile of deserted furniture, she said to no one, "He's dead." Though he was still poking about in a warped armoire, he silently agreed.

Because she knew he wasn't there, Mrs. Michaels could see her husband more clearly in the space he had abandoned, and she no longer called to or searched for him. Instead, she noticed his absence beside her in the morning, the blankets smooth on his side of the bed. She remembered how he would pretend to be still asleep so she could wash up before him and she rose with pleasure and walked to the bathroom. Next to her hovered Mr. Michaels, who, unable to know her thoughts, saw only her satisfaction and felt more than invisible: forgotten. He watched her morning ritual for the first time, as she washed her face and pressed soapy fingers into the wrinkles with determination, as she combed her thin gray hair carefully, the curls twisting as they slipped through the dark plastic teeth. A strand fell to the floor and Mr. Michaels wished he could catch it. But it was yet another small, private moment of his wife's that had passed him invisibly all his life and that now, in death, couldn't be held. And when she began to pull up her nightgown to sit on the toilet, he had to look away.

After dressing, Mrs. Michaels walked downstairs, remembering her husband by the lack of his morning cough, by not hearing him humming while he opened and closed the drawers and closet door. In the kitchen she filled the cereal bowl with flakes of bran, poking among them and counting the number of raisins. Her unhappy husband counted along with her, amazed at the deftness of her fingers, yet lonely as she poured the milk into the bowl and smiled at his empty place.

When his wife left to go to the market, Mr. Michaels called to the closing door, "Please, come back!" but she didn't hear. He was afraid to follow, certain that he'd float away in the wind outside, and when she returned he attended her movements even more closely. In the evening, as Mrs. Michaels sat in the tub's cloudy water and carefully untangled the hair under her arms after sponging off the soap, she felt a chill of wind on her back while her husband attempted to knead her stiff shoulders with his invisible fingers.

One night in bed Mrs. Michaels' hands began to travel, palms lingering at the rise of hips. Her fingers probed, tentatively, to a distant past. Eyes closed, she saw her husband much younger, his hair still thick and dark. Mr. Michaels, hovering in bed beside her, watched her hands moving with grace and he couldn't turn away and grant her this private act. Instead, he floated over and drifted gently down upon her. He tried to move his airy body in the ways he thought she was imagining while her hands called up memories of his elbows by her arms, his lips at her forehead. When her body finally shook and settled, he remained over her, a transparent blanket in the dark. Then she pulled up the covers and he curled into the folds. He could hear the leaves falling in the wind outside and he imagined they were words he whispered to his wife, to which she responded by half-turning, her thin legs against him. In her unsettled sleep she dreamt she was a child chasing something she couldn't see, growing older with every stride she took. Yet for him, always awake, the darkness was now a kind of sleep, her rustlings under the blanket a kind of dream.

He rose in the middle of the night and glided to the window, where the furious whistling of the wind surged against the glass. He watched the brown twisting leaves scuttle over the black lawn, and when his wife rose from the bed, drawn as well to the wind, he imagined that she knew he was beside the window. Slowly, awkwardly at first, she hummed along with the insistent, then muted flourishes outside and he joined her, trying with his transparent voice to harmonize. In their own ways they followed the turns of an ancient music, Mrs. Michaels in her white nightgown, accompanied by her lover, her invisible husband.

The Distance

At night we lie curled together, yet in the morning we're on opposite sides of the bed. At first we thought this merely midnight drift. And in fact, you confess to dreaming that you dedicated a ship that had my name and, with champagne foam on the prow, it churned out to sea without you. I dreamt I planted a seed that grew so fast I hadn't even finished watering it when I was caught in its branches, on its insanely swift climb to the sky. And I called your name, vainly.

Yes, we say, as we gaze at each other across the distance of sheets, midnight drift.

Perhaps not, we think, holding our small daughter as we stand at the top of the stairs and stare down to the first floor, which seems so far away. And when we climb down, really *jump* from one level to another, we think perhaps it's merely the sunrise crawl. Indeed, you feel queasy, as if standing at the end of a gently swaying pier, watching a ship shrink in the distance. And these jumps remind me of leaping from branch to branch, on a tree that is growing faster than I can climb down.

Yet we do make it downstairs. Even so, we begin to feel

it's not the drift, it's not the crawl; instead we return to our old fear that you and I have been living in this house too long, and everything seems to be outgrowing us.

Because during breakfast we have to strain to lift the spoons, which feel as heavy as shovels. When we lift them we see the reflection of our heads—inverted and huge. Confronted with the enormous bowls, we pour in the huge flakes of Wheaties and Post Toasties. Yet for all the milk we add, when we look at the still half-filled bowls our appetites disappear. And we're only left with a taste of our dreams fading in our mouths.

The telephone rings. Only then do we notice that the rug in the living room now reaches up to our knees, and it's impossible to get from one end of the room to the other before the tenth, final bell. As the bitter sound of that last ring dies away, we hear our young daughter crying. We look back into the kitchen: her highchair is empty. She must have followed us and is now lost somewhere in the thickest pile of the rug. Yet no matter how closely we search, pushing away at this insistent fog of carpet and calling in return, her cries always seem to be in the distance. And because the rug is even taller now, as desperate as we are and knowing how much more ground we could cover each on our own, we don't dare separate.

By now the telephone on the wall is out of reach. There's no longer any possibility of climbing to the latch of the screen door, and even if we could we'd only succeed in letting the cat in. Its food dish *is* empty. The parakeet is also hungry. While it jumps from cage bar to perch and back again, squawking, eyeing every move we make, I can only hope it starves before it learns how to break out of its cage.

Squawks, growls, crying: it seems everywhere we turn, we're stalemated. There's nothing left to do but pray that the rest of the neighborhood notices just how much our house is outgrowing us. How can they ignore the sides of our house, which are growing into their yards, overturning the birdbath, destroying the shrubs? How can they ignore our roof, which blocks the noonday sun?

We hold each other tighter, though already you look at me as if I were a speck on the horizon, and when I whisper your name it sounds like a shout in the distance. Yet we don't let go: perhaps we can only move into each other while the rest of the house moves farther away. I begin to unbutton your blouse and you unbutton my shirt, sadly, tenderly, as if for the last time. I look over your shoulder in a vain attempt to include the house in our passion: my eyes mimic the movement of your hands and follow like buttons the knobs of the distant dresser drawer up to the top. Up to where the window, with its clear brilliance, beckons like an invitation.

There's no other choice. Drawing upon more endurance than we thought we ever had, we begin the ascent— slippery round knob by slippery round knob. Each one, it appears, is a little larger, a little farther away than the last.

Finally at the top, we look out the window and there in the distance, across from us, staring back at us through their own incredibly huge window, are our neighbors: little postage stamps misplaced on a gigantic letter that will never be delivered. We slowly wave to each other while below, the cats begin to howl.

IV

The Art of the Knock: Two

It was the hottest day of the year and I was getting nowhere in a miserable little one-tree town. I couldn't sell anything, not the six-handled, multijointed Family Fork, not the Adjustable Headache with music box timer, not even the ever popular Memory Lane Mirror. The doors of those steaming houses just wouldn't open, not even a crack, despite the fact that my knuckles were tapping like a dripping faucet, rolling like ice cubes in a tall, cool glass, even flowing like a cold waterfall! No, all those sweating customers suffered in private while the dogs inside barked at me through the mail slots. The neighborhood started to seem miles long in the heat, the houses becoming so gigantic that one glance at a huge door was enough to stop and set me trudging off to the next behemoth down the road. But it seemed so far away that the courage I'd cranked up to knock on the door collapsed by the time I got there!

Finally, I sat under the only tree in town and released my entire line of Pint o' Fresh Air into the sky. Then I took the empty bottles and began to collect shade. I scooped up a dark patch that was hiding under the crook of a twisted, exposed tree root. I shook a branch and then let the shade fall from the leaves into a large jar. I spent two hours with a tweezers, picking the shade from under a foraging ant. But I soon felt sorry for the little creature as it repeatedly and frantically scanned the ground with its antennae whenever its shadow briefly vanished. So I stopped. It wasn't necessary to fill that bottle, I realized, for here I had a kind of caviar. And in any case, I could always claim the contents had settled during shipment. Finally capping all the bottles, I turned each one around in my hand, watched the coolness swirl about and observed, *in broad daylight,* the patterns of evening that only lacked the stars. I tried to think of a name for my new product.

Meanwhile a mail carrier walked down the block, pushing his letters in the mailboxes and through the slots, and leaving packages by the doors. *And those doors opened,* the same stubborn ones I'd cracked my knuckles against. I stood staring in amazement and the bottle I was holding slipped from my fingers: its shade spilled through the broken glass and quickly withered under the glare of the sun. And I'd thought I knew doors. How wrong I had been. That night, I dreamt I was walking toward a door that hid every shadow in the world. I stood and pounded until the hinges loosened and my knuckles were white from knocking. The door itself turned white, becoming a giant envelope, and with each additional rap the words of a letter gleamed within. . . .

I woke up the next morning prepared to change my life. Here was my chance for a sure glimpse inside every house— I'd push a product that couldn't be refused! Why, I'd be gifted with a handful of letters *and* my varied knock, and grateful homeowners would gladly open their doors and welcome me in. I'd become a daily addition to their homes, the happy, prodigal son who arrives again and again. Determined to sweep and scrub my career and then redecorate, I checked out from the dump where I was staying and I dragged along my merchandise, every last little industrial gesture I had on me. I was going to get rid of it all, though I didn't have an easy time with this decision. I'd grown fond of the Automatic Door Slammer, the Refrigerator Alarm, the Guilt Remover (with complimentary applicator), the Conjugal Bed Tollbooth, and more, each one complete with a memory that followed my resolve reluctantly, kicking and screaming, not wanting to die.

But I couldn't just leave those lovely products alone on a street corner, or desert them at the gate of an orphanage. No, I knew if I left my past life in the lurch it would never forgive me, and the *last* thing I needed was a few of my former decades plotting revenge. I had to find a new home for every cubic inch of inventory and then bow out gracefully with no forwarding address. So I thought I'd give everything away, no funny stuff: *What's that, ma'am? You'd like a Negligee Night-light? Here you are, it's yours, free of charge. Enjoy it.* So I stood with my suitcases open, ready to part with my entire stock to any passing stranger. But it was no use: all my offers were met with silence and quickening steps, and when a patrol car slowly passed by I decided to pack up my good intentions before I was hauled in and charged with attempted generosity.

It was then that I felt like one of my prospective customers: even *I* didn't want any of my products! But where was *my* door to slam, where was the insistent, solid "goodbye" that would shed all my troubles? Perhaps I should have left my wares at a bus stop curb and let the automatic doors hiss shut behind me, my new home driving me far away. But as I walked along I came upon a refuse truck rumbling by the sidewalk. It was chewing up all of an evicted family's discarded household remains that the garbage men threw to it. What better way to mash my missed chances? I thought, and I slipped my suitcases on top of a dirty refrigerator without a door, its pale, white interior exposed to an alien climate. Soon I saw my baggage shoved into the truck, and that grinding mouth crushed every last particle of my former profession. I walked away a new and empty man.

So I joined the postal service, and I tore through my training as if it were an anxiously awaited letter. First they had me collect the ingredients for stamp glue. Every morning, before the sun even came close to kissing the curve of the horizon, I rose and searched in the darkest wooded corners for the bitter forest herbs that were listed in the postal catalog. But I outdid them and specialized in my own field trips to discover new and nastier flavors. I recovered the baked insect remains off of city streetlamps. I collected sidewalk scrapings after an acid rain. I suctioned off the hand sweat from hospital emergency-room doorknobs. My triumph, however, was the night I sat in the last speeding, twisting seat and with an extremely fine screen caught the condensed breath of the screaming rollercoaster riders. I did so well that there was even talk of promoting me to the laboratory where junk mail is grown and crossbred. But I had other plans: I wanted a mail run. I wanted to get back to those doors.

That first morning, as I gathered the packets of mail and slipped them like little sleeping creatures into my pouch, I contemplated what a perfect product is the letter. Such crisp edges, such a clean, white facade! Each upper right corner is graced with a tiny work of art, though just what it might be is never predictable: perhaps a famous president, a rare bird, an industrial giant, or a multicolored flag. Ah, the letter—a monument to stability, a salute to variability! The senders' names and addresses, which are always different, sit in the upper left-hand corner, which is always the same. And in the center lie the ever changing names and addresses of the recipients. Yet they're really our *customers,* for every sale is assured—the letter is irresistible. Why, it seems to mail itself! It crosses state borders with ease, silent as a knife, and each envelope is a beckoning surprise, holding its paper-thin blade of joy or despair inside, just waiting to cut through the reader's calm exterior.

So I walked from the post office in my lovely blue uniform, my letters snug in my sack, and I was certain of success. I walked slowly, savoring each step that was leading me to my bright and flaring future: for I was about to enter the land of the Sure Thing. And then, there I was: before the first house on my route. I could see that those moony glass eyes on that solid face would never betray the door, with its knob a gleaming nub that reflected every approaching finger. I walked up the walk, I ascended the short steps, and then I knocked with a simple series of fingertaps, gentle as a baby's first clutching grasp.

I waited. A face peered through a crack between the curtains. Then the door opened slightly until its inside chain held it tight. A voice from the darkness said, "Yes?"

"Your mail." I held it all before me.

"My mail."

"Yes, don't you want it?" I asked, and I extended my full hand, my first delivery! But before I could extol the postal virtues, a flash of fingers cleaned me out and the door locked with a sharp click.

Hmmmm, I thought, I'm new here: *that* must be the problem. For on every street, at every house, I stood before a dark doorway slit, a dim face, and then a supersonic hand swooped out and stripped me of my mail while my first words, unable to break the sound barrier, withered in my mouth. Then, on my last block, a huge woman with a face as flat and wide as a pasture opened the door, looked me over from my polished shoes to my jaunty cap with its crisp brim, daintily took each letter from me, and said, "Tomorrow, just put the mail in the mailbox. Don't knock."

My fingertips twitched and trembled, as if about to jump from my hands in surprise. And then there I stood again, alone before a shut door. I must not have heard right, I thought. But as I trudged back to the post office, I began to think that perhaps it was my knock that was all wrong— *it needed to connect with the contents of the letters.* The next morning, as I collected my packets, I applied to every individual envelope the delicate touch of my fingertips, hoping to pressure myself into the ink-bound secrets inside. If the news was happy, why, I could give a cloudless knock, the blue skies reflected in my every fingernail! If the news was sad, I could give a mourning knock, each finger a weeping tear bunched into a knot of sorrow. But it was no use: I had no idea if Granny's Fido had died, or if Daddy's lottery ticket had blossomed. I was lost in the whorl of my fingerprints; I was cut off from both the shriek of delight in my rapping and the melancholy news of my knuckles. Those envelopes, those thin white ghosts of trees, those tiny, failed doors, sat silent in my palm.

So that was the life I saw before me: I'd be a go-between, delivering twenty-cent foreplay to spineless stamp lickers. Stunned by my shortened sights, I sadly walked through my neighborhood of mailboxes, leaving letters, my sack slowly lightening and my poor, dazed hands not even dumb show, my knuckles mere bumps on my forlorn fists. Every door stayed shut, the interior of each house still a mystery, and I began to wish I could mail myself a world away, where I could be opened up and read with delight and understanding.

The Art of the Knock: Two

One day, sheltered from a rainstorm in an alley with an umbrella of junk mail in my hand, I contemplated violating the glued edges and white borders of that third-class mail. And yes, soon after the storm passed, a circle of crumpled and gaping envelopes lay at my feet. But what did I find inside? An auto repair center advertising, with intimations of honest work, its new "Lubritorium"; an exterminating company giving tongue to the secret of its latest, low-priced poison; a footwear firm plugging its Almost-Leather products; an insurance company proclaiming a comprehensive Annoying-Next-Door-Neighbor policy; the Instant Institute offering a "Kwik Kourse in Psychiatry"; and much, much more. I could just see vast amounts of this stuff piled up in the garbage bin of every house, unopened or ripped in half and then torn in pieces just for the fun of it. *This* was what I was carrying around on my bent back—not even my past, beloved products, but their mere echoes encased in printed patter?

Suicide seemed one way out of my career dilemma. If I jumped off a building my hands could flail against the air, making thousands of tiny knocks until I finally balled into a giant, final fist and smashed against my last door, the ground! I could lie on a track until a train flattened me like a spread palm on the surface of a door. I could even slit my throat, but then how would my hands knock while they tried to hold exploding veins? No, even though my knuckles were now strangers to a hard surface, my fingers failures at friction, I *needed* my knock: a gentle and passionate lover that can flirt with a door more ways than can be counted. But how could I return to my memories and market them again? No more would I be an intermediary: I was sick of smoke; I wanted to be the attracting flame. I finally realized that *I was on the wrong side of the door.* But where was *my* door, where was someone else's knock, and where was my echo inside?

V

Light Bulbs

Mother and Father seldom hear from the children. Their daughter, living alone in Asia, writes letters in a calligraphy so beautiful that they have stopped having them translated. Instead, Mother laminates them for use as place mats. The graceful characters enhance the irregular swirls of spilled gravy, the random drips of coffee. And the twins, who recently swapped spouses and are fighting over custody of their children, rarely call.

Home remains quiet. Mother and Father never were great talkers and they still aren't; they keep busy in other ways. Mother continues to knit her afghan for the children—each knitted row another line of a sad, undelivered letter that has long since grown out of the sewing room and lies in neat folds along the sides of the hall. Father continues to repair the abandoned toys, remembering with amusement how the twins would insist on identical toys and how they would always break them in the same way. Now the old playroom seems like a convalescent home, where fewer and fewer visitors come. Waiting for the return of something they perhaps can't name, Mother and Father keep the curtains open in the evenings and all the lights on. Sometimes they stand together at the bay window and stare out at an impenetrable darkness—a darkness like a photographic negative, which reflects back their lonely, peering faces.

Lately, the light bulbs have begun to go out in an unpredictable and alarming way—in the study, over the stairwell, in the middle of a recipe in the kitchen. Some nights, Mother and Father have to stalk from room to room, fresh bulbs in hand, seeking to transform every dim corner. From the outside, their home seems to have a nervous blink.

Father finds himself attracted to the sound of the bulbs as they go out—some with a kind of smoky burst, some with a faint, regretful pop. It's as if they all had their own secret reasons for leaving. He also can't avoid noticing the way the old bulbs fit into the palm of his hand like the warm head of an infant. Father keeps this to himself. He has begun to spend more of his time at night watching the lights and less with Mother at the bay window.

Father stands in the hallway, peering around a bookcase, waiting for a room to be enveloped in darkness. When it happens, he untwists the bulb and listens to the death rattle of its tiny filament. He stares at its pale face, dimly lit from the next room, and notes the smudgy bruise on its forehead: a fatal inner injury. Then he holds the bulb up to his ear in an attempt to hear any last words. Mother watches him from a corner. She follows him from room to room. She notices how he replaces each used bulb with a fresh one from his supply. "Soon," she murmurs to herself, "all the lights in the house will be his."

One night, when Father returns to the bay window, Mother isn't there. He calls her name, but there is no answer. Almost without knowing it, he feels a satisfaction slipping away inside him. He hurries down the halls, peering into every doorway. There, in the bedroom, standing on a chair, replacing a ceiling light with one of her own, is Mother.

"What are you doing?" Father cries out.

"I don't trust your light bulbs," she replies.

After this, Mother and Father avoid each other. They brood in separate rooms, each of them alone with a single lamp and its sympathetic light. Quietly, without formal declaration, they agree to split the house between them. Father claims the study, the guest room, the twins' bedroom, the playroom, the basement, and half of the hallways. Mother claims the master bedroom, their daughter's bedroom, the dining room, the living room, the attic, and the other half of the hallways. The bathrooms are disputed and the kitchen is neutral.

Days pass and the mail accumulates. Bills, catalogs, and even a beautiful letter from overseas lie unopened on the kitchen table. Father spends his afternoons in the basement, where he attempts to repair the broken bulbs. The useless vacuum, the trapped filament, the untouchable interior all serve to hold him at bay. When he inspects his rooms in the evenings, he half-hopes he won't find still another lifeless bulb to add to his defeats.

Mother continues to knit. When a bulb dies with a silent sigh in one of her rooms she rushes to it with open palms, unscrews it, and then carries it to the afghan, which now lies along her side of the hallway. Her sad, used bulbs are tucked under the folds of the blanket, with the names she has painted on their foreheads: Buzzy, Janet, Spencer, Darlene, Kevin, Tia—names she always wanted to give to children she never had. Now Mother places the latest— Charles—under the warm fold. When she tucks him in, he stays tucked: a little sleeper who will never awake.

Father, far from content, begins to plan sabotage. In the afternoons, while Mother nods over her latest stretch of afghan, Father untwists her bulbs slightly in the sockets until they go out. Later, drowsy but then anxious, she hurries to replace them, not noticing Father's trick. In the evening, Father switches his used bulbs, his failed patients, for the good ones that Mother has unwittingly laid to rest under the blanket. In this way, Father begins to light his rooms with her bulbs. One afternoon Mother dreams that her little sleepers are restless, rattling their filaments as they doze. But she wakes to see it is Father, unscrewing one of her bulbs. Mother is startled, but remains silent. "Soon," she whispers to herself, no longer fooled, "all the bulbs in the house will be mine."

But this plan fails too. When lit, Mother's painted bulbs begin to melt their names, which, drop by drop, gather in puddles on lamp stands, chairs, and rugs. Father stares for a long time at the stains, difficult script of another language. Though disappointed, Father now launches further raids on Mother's territory, searching for broken bulbs, bulbs without names. Mother, her half-closed eyes ever alert, keeps watch through her nap. When he passes down the hall, she lays aside her knitting and, bulbs in hand, explores his dark rooms. Father hears her light footsteps overhead, in the study. Like Mother, he now begins to understand that each bulb could be a friend or an enemy. Boundaries disappear, and Father and Mother enter the rooms like guerrillas, ever on the alert.

One night, the light in the playroom goes out, and Mother and Father arrive there at the same instant, through different doors. Each convinced that the other is about to seize the dead bulb and twist it from its socket, they circle each other in the dark, crushing toy soldiers and porcelain dolls under their feet. Little wooden helmets and tiny, unblinking glass eyes roll about on the floor. Mother and Father try to step around these as they tiptoe silently, listening for the dry squeak of a turning bulb.

The phone rings. Who could it be? One of the twins?

Gripping their bulbs tighter, Mother and Father each wait for the other to break and run to the telephone. Perhaps it's long distance from their daughter! Both Mother and Father are close to giving in, when the ringing stops, just before the tenth bell. Mother and Father stand very still, facing each other, eyes now accustomed to the darkness. The bulb above them waits patiently in its socket. They each take two steps forward, and then, without speaking, Father lifts Mother up and she replaces their bulb.

Now Father and Mother live silently together. They have disconnected the phone, they continue to leave the mail unopened, and they do not answer the doorbell. Mother and Father are busy with their bulbs. Mother knits shades for all the lamps in the house, choosing a different stitch for each—a special pattern of light on every wall. Father builds cabinets to hold the new bulbs—a honeycomb of unborn lights. Now when a bulb goes out, the feeling for Mother and Father is bittersweet: the gift of light has given way to the gift of darkness. When the bulb over the dining room table goes off, right in the middle of dessert, the last few spoons of tapioca seem to taste better in the dark. Then they rise and take that bulb slowly out of its socket, Mother standing on a chair and Father holding the chair steady. They place the still-warm bulb in a potholder Mother specially knitted, and together they climb the stairs to the attic.

Once there, they open a large hope chest. Even in the dimness they can see rows and rows of bulbs laid to rest. Mother and Father stand quietly a few moments, respecting each other's thoughts. Then they carefully place the bulb with its companions. The new addition sends a staggered chorus of sympathetic clicks throughout the rows of bulbs, and this slight song is heard by Mother and Father long after they close the hope chest and descend the stairs to their brightly lit rooms.

Waiting for the
Right Moment

They met one afternoon at a Japanese restaurant, strangers side by side at the hibachi table. He was intent upon the last grains of rice in his bowl; she, alone and bored while waiting to order, was taken by his look of concentration and listened to the awkward yet musical clicks of his chopsticks. The lantern behind him luminously framed his face, and she began quietly fashioning his features in origami from the cigarette pack she'd just finished. After he cleaned out his bowl he turned and discovered her just as she was finishing the line of his jaw, the Surgeon General's warning jutting out at an odd angle. When she saw him staring at her she embarrassed herself by blurting out, "It's you."

His forehead wrinkled and he stared at the cigarette pack, unsure of her meaning. Afraid he was offended, she quickly added, "Cubism becomes you." He smiled. The monosodium glutamate was beginning to affect him. Yes, he thought, sometimes I feel like that. Though he'd finished his meal, he ordered a bottle of plum wine, which they shared; and over the nearby sizzling of steak strips and bean sprouts they made their acquaintance.

The Art of the Knock

She was an artist, she said, though she worked as an assistant to a designer of new pasta shapes. Her office building, two blocks away, was not very far from the law firm where he worked, filing suit against toy manufacturers for the parents of maimed children. "Every department-store toy shelf," he said, "has a dangerous product lying in wait for a child."

"I have nothing but customers lying in wait for *my* work," she laughed. "A new pasta creation is a work of art, but once it's eaten, it's gone. What kind of artist can destroy a successful canvas?"

She spoke of some of her recent pasta forms and he listened closely, happy to be in a world far from tiny, unpredictable plastic propellers and splinter-prone doll houses. For both of them, the sweetness of the plum wine filled their mouths with an unspoken anticipation, and they agreed to meet the next day for lunch in the park.

He sat in his apartment that evening and turned the cigarette pack over in his palm while his other hand traced the line of his ears, nose, cheeks, and temples. If all his fingers were broken, he thought, their touch against his face might resemble that paper bust; or if he were a fly the thousands of lenses in his eyes might create a similar view. He finally grew tired of examining, from every direction, her interpretation of his angles, but he slept little that night, as if his bed had suddenly developed unexpected ridges and valleys. Across town she sat on her bed, surrounded by hundreds of untouched cigarettes, the discarded contents of an entire carton. She folded and trimmed the empty packs in an effort to improve upon her work of the afternoon. Shortly after she had gone through the carton she fell asleep, her arms cradling a crowd of twisted paper faces.

The next day, holding orange drinks and frankfurters,

they walked along park paths that were nearly empty from the threat of approaching rain clouds. The wind blew small bare branches down from the trees while he talked to her of his college days and confessed that he had wanted to be an art historian. She bent down to grab a pair of twigs that were skimming across the path before them. He hadn't been able to decide, he continued, between specializing in the postimpressionists and modern sculpture between the wars. She smiled and carefully pulled a loose branch from a bush. He said that when he had realized how many foreign languages he would have had to learn for an advanced degree, he had regretfully decided to go into law instead. She nodded sympathetically. Soon she had an armful of broken branches and he was balancing the food he now held for both of them, when she asked to have lunch together for the next day. "Of course," he said, and they walked along in the soft rain.

He was waiting outside her office building the following afternoon when she appeared through the revolving door holding what he at first thought was a giant pretzel. As she came closer he saw it was the branches she'd gathered the day before, lacquered and twisted further into the shape of a face. She held it before her and its outlines matched her own features, her eyes and lips filling the curves of polished wood. She watched him through it, his face framed also and a look of recognition in his eyes.

From then on they saw each other often. During the day, as he sat in court making motions for eye-patched victims of pop-up storybooks or to initiate a massive recall of defective tricycles, he would anticipate the coming evening, when she would meet him with her latest works, usually simple, private mementos. With gentle, admiring glances he regarded them all: a tiny mobile of birdlike figures, made from the ticket stubs of movies they'd seen together; small, suggestive pendants carved from wooden ice-cream spoons; a set of snapshots of restaurant table legs where their feet had touched in the past. She wanted her work to be an antidote to his slow days surrounded by depressing, dangerous toys, while he found himself quietly posing for her, hoping to influence her inspiration, but her work of art the next day always surprised him. Once, before an evening of theater, they decided to have dinner at an out-of-the-way restaurant recommended by her boss, but on the way they got completely lost. Her next work was a painting: a map of the city, with key routes tapering off to nowhere and street names misplaced across town from their real homes, a maze of mistakes in every direction. The time they spent together always seemed to have a hidden gift that became her newest creation, a shared secret that entwined itself around them.

After one sun-filled late morning of their arms and legs twisting and uncoiling on the couch, he went to the kitchen to make lunch while she went to his study. There she looked through his collection of broken toys, exhibits from his past cases: a kerosine-fed miniature volcano, a doll that grew sharpened fingernails at the press of a button, a motorized jumping rope, shelf upon shelf of tidy ruins. She picked out pieces here and there and with a pile of parts, plus a paperweight from his desk, she sat down on the floor and began to tinker away. Just as he was about to fold the eggs into an omelet she came into the kitchen and handed him the prototype of her windup prism. The moment he saw it, he was pleased she'd dismantled his morbid collection. He placed it on the floor, turned the key, and the wheels set off in erratic curves, the crystal surfaces ecstatically reflecting the afternoon light against every corner of the room, as if revealing all his hidden facets.

A week later, they were putting up on his living room

wall her silk screen of their fingerprints, larger than life-size and joined in a series of increasingly acrobatic positions, when she murmured in his ear, "You are my gallery." He imagined himself reproduced all over his apartment, the center of her art. That decided him. He asked her to move in.

It was then that her work really began to develop, her inspiration bursting out at the oddest hours. He woke on and off one night, aware of the smell of paste, the clip of scissors, and the rustling of paper. In the morning he found the bed covered with the shambles of *GQ* and *U.S. News & World Report*. She was stretched out by the bedposts, red-eyed and still working. "You talk in your sleep," she murmured, and indeed, her collage was of his sleeping figure, filled with paragraph after paragraph of last night's confessions. He leaned over and examined every line, amazed to be reading about events he only remembered in his dreams. Near the outline of the left elbow was an account from his childhood, when he had secretly watched his mother carefully apply false nails to her fingers and then tenderly stroke his absent father's spare wig. By the rib cage was a nightmare: though an adult, he was lost in a monkey-bars that multiplied beyond his range of vision. He finally rose from the bed, feeling entangled in his own pajamas, and walked to the bathroom. There, when he opened the medicine cabinet, an Instamatic flashed in his face. It was the beginning of her continuing photographic series, titled *Searching for Toothpaste*. He blinked and rubbed his eyes, a small price, he thought, for the cause of art.

She was now working only part-time in pasta. In the former guest room there gradually appeared a pottery wheel, piles of canvas and stretchers, tubes of paint, stone blocks, chisels, fabrics, a loom, two cameras, and rolls of film. There seemed to be no part of his life that didn't inspire her: the way his socks on the floor curled like a passionate couple, how he opened and closed the air vents with an almost tender regard, even the way his handwriting looped at odd angles between the thin straight lines of his notebook caught her glance. Soon her art began to multiply in the apartment, even in the most unlikely places. He was working on a current case, an injunction against a proposed product—Home Graffiti, with nontoxic, disappearing spray paint—when he opened his desk drawer for some scrap paper and found that everything inside had been replaced by gleaming ceramic replicas of a note pad, a pencil sharpener, paper clips, pens and pen-tops, and an eraser. There were even a number of ceramic coins, accurate down to the dates, totaling eighty-three cents. But he still had no paper. Annoyed, he turned to look around the room for some small scrap he might use, when he saw her standing in the doorway. She was holding a leather-bound notebook in the shape of his profile. "I thought you might need a replacement," she said, smiling.

Almost daily a surprise awaited him in the apartment. Dressing for work one morning, he found his shoes and hers nailed to a parquet board and arranged in a series of dance steps, the laces and straps lacquered and raised in the air, in the pose of arms softly brushing one another. "Do you like it?" she shouted from the kitchen. "It's called *Light on Their Feet.*" He did like it, imagining both of them toe to toe in a darkened room. But now, after her raid on his shoes, all he had left to wear to work was a pair of jogging sneakers he'd never used. He felt ridiculous in them with his business suit, and a block before his office he entered a shoe store and bought two new pairs.

They had their first argument that evening. "I'm no lover," he complained, "I'm an art shop, supplying you with materials."

"Not at all, love," she replied. "You supply inspiration. The shoes are extra."

He started to shout. She refused to listen and left the room. He followed her until she slammed the bathroom door in his face. He was left alone in the hall, surrounded by the series of photographs of him half-asleep and startled in his pajamas. She sat alone and unhappy beneath the bathroom sink, her cheek against the cold silver pipe that connected to the ground. She wanted to throw bottles of hand cream and bath oil against the shower tiles, but instead she just imagined the stains they might make, and she thought of how she could make the stains into something beautiful, something that might delight him. An hour later she presented him with a drawing of two wrestling ink blots, the designs trailing off in all directions to a thin shower of specks and dots. As he held it in his hands he felt his anger fade away too.

Within a week he found the drawing framed and on the wall of his study. The rooms of the apartment continued to fill up with her work and she spent more time than ever in the studio. One evening she even worked behind a closed door while he sat on the living room couch, going over a brief for his latest case: an animal maze—Little Behaviorist—that so frustrated the mice (not included) that they bit the children handling them. He was tired and, idly glancing about him, he noticed that the cushion his arm was resting on was actually a soft sculpture of his Social Security card. Suddenly he had an attack of claustrophobia. Another work of art, he thought, and the apartment would burst like an overstuffed closet. He walked over to the studio door and entered without knocking. There she was in the center of the room, surrounded by a litter of flood lights, zoom lenses, rolls of film, and a collection of her latest work.

"Another series?" he asked in despair.

"No," she replied, surprised at his sudden entrance. "I'm taking pictures for the catalog of my first showing."

"A showing!" he exclaimed, forgetting his anger. "Why didn't you tell me before?"

"I wanted to surprise you."

"Where's it going to be?"

"Here."

He drank more than he should have during the reception. This made it difficult for him to sign the copy of the catalog thrust in his face by a woman who cornered him near the makeshift bar. "You're the real star, the inspiration of the best work here." She lowered her voice. "I can have an exhibition ready in Washington by September. It'll be called 'Realism: Super to Three-dimensional.' You, of course, would be the apotheosis of the entire event." He spilled his drink before he could reply, making a series of teary streaks down the front of his suit. "Effortless," she said. "You're without any self-consciousness. Art simply clings to you."

The show was a success, described by notices as "witty and eclectic," "an open house of art," and "an unprecedented combination of apartment, studio, gallery, and lover," with only one dissenting review: "a mutant page ripped from *Good Housekeeping*." Buyers were interested, and she put her work up for sale; pasta was now a thing of the past. Soon familiar objects began to disappear. Coming home from work one day he saw that the closet door, which had been covered with a bas-relief of his dental X rays, was gone. "I sold it this morning," she explained and gently led him away from the exposed rack of suits. "Don't worry. I'll do a new one," she said. Later, while he angrily made notes for the next day's deposition against a toy grenade that actually exploded into allegedly harmless rubber shrapnel, she sat in her workroom and tried to imagine a new door that would almost beg a hand to open it.

While old works vanished, others appeared. A sculpture of his hands, the fingers spread apart in a gesture of flight, was gone, replaced by a pottery urn, empty and titled *Without Ashes.* On the bedroom wall, where a multiple-perspective sketch of his key chain had once been, there was now a watercolor of his receding hairline. Though he was happy for her success, with every sale he felt taken apart, *divided* into works of art, and he had no control over where he might be displayed. She was always working. The dust from chiseled stone speckled her hair, patches of oil paint stained her fingers, and modeling clay caked beneath her nails. With the constant rush of new art he found himself in rooms he could now barely recognize and he would glance about nervously, as if he were in someone else's home and about to be discovered.

Finally one night he awoke in the early hours and saw that she'd left the bed. He got up and quietly searched for her, thinking perhaps she was working. By the light of the moon from the window he found her, in the living room, with *Light on Their Feet,* the one work she had repeatedly refused to sell. Her bare feet were fit into a pair of her dancing shoes, opposite one of his empty pairs. Her eyes were closed and she was smiling as her shining body swayed before an invisible partner. He returned to bed unseen and so disturbed that he didn't notice when she came back to lie beside him. When his feet finally stopped twitching he fell asleep—with his fist in his mouth, afraid of what he might reveal of his dreams.

He woke before the alarm and left the apartment while she still slept. On the walk from the subway station to his office he passed a shoe store. He stopped and stared at the rows of loafers, boots, casuals, high heels, and slippers that faced him silently. For lunch he went back to the Japanese restaurant where they'd first met. It was early and the tables were mostly empty. He sat alone, watching the chef sharpen his knives one against the other. Later, while he waited for the check, the restaurant filling up, he stared at the seat beside him, still empty.

Returning home that evening, he opened the door and stood there, hesitant, then frightened, for he saw stretched out on the living room floorboards by the window a life-size painting of a shadow. "It's your shadow," she said as she came up to kiss him hello and lead him into the room, "I just finished work on it." It was titled *Waiting for the Right Moment.* One day, she explained, he'd pass by the window and, given the correct lighting, moment, and identical gesture, his shadow would match, for an instant, the painted one. His feet tingled as he stood uneasily at the edge of the flat, dark shape. "It's only a matter of time," she said.

Twins

Soon after I was born my parents bitterly divorced, and they divided up their possessions with a relentless energy, hoping to impel themselves from each other with such force that they would never be drawn back again. I have always imagined that they made two great, equal piles in each room as they sorted in a rage through everything in the house, from the curtains and large sets of furniture to the knickknacks in the kitchen drawers. When they were done, only their two small sons were left and, for reasons that even now they cannot adequately express, they divided us up as well. Father took Paul, my twin brother, and Mother kept me. We were just a year old at the time, a single child conveniently doubled for that terrible, wrenching split.

As I grew up all that I knew of Paul was his name, though I could faintly remember once chasing, as if after myself, a toddler who wore the same clothes as I. If this wasn't a memory, I had surely made it up from longing, for I was always bumping into the empty space of my absent brother with my small, chubby body. When I sat on the couch watching TV and eating an entire bag of potato chips, I pretended Paul was sitting beside me, asking me for some chips or to change the channel. I refused, of course, and we would then argue in the nagging manner of other brothers whom I had observed. Or I went outside and threw a tennis ball against the garage wall and imagined we were playing catch. I became my brother and aimed the ball at the edges of the shingles, making it bounce back at an odd angle, and as myself I caught it skillfully. Yet when my mother called me in to dinner there were only two place settings, not three. I sat lonely at the table and watched Mother shift the pots and pans on the stove. When she turned around to fill the plates with food she squinted, for she never wore her glasses when we ate, claiming that the steam from the hot food clouded them up. But I often wondered if, with her glasses off, Mother saw double and I became both twins eating before her. Perhaps that was why she fed me so much and so often—to sustain that vision.

I had learned not to ask Mother about my father, for her silence on this matter was worse than any shouted, angry refusal, and I was forced to invent him as well. I saw him as tall, with a cruel, pointed hairline, and he wore the kind of suit with painfully sharp creases that mannequins modeled in shop windows. If I tripped on the basement steps or bumped my head against the freezer in the refrigerator, I would hear his disembodied laughter, his pleasure at my misfortune. And at night, with the gray, frightening forms of furniture around me, I tried to understand why my parents had left each other. Though now I believe they simply began treating each other as poorly as they secretly treated themselves, during those lonely nights I conjured up outlandish quarrels, full of desperate acts and hurled objects, between the mother I knew and the father I imagined.

Left with my own insufficient memory and my mother's pervasive silence, occasionally during the day I examined the furniture in each room and tried to decipher the house's secret scars. What had been taken away to Father's distant home and then replaced, and what had stayed? While gnawing on some snack I circled the dining room table and its surrounding chairs; I fingered the plates and the silverware that framed them; I spread my hands across the recliner and accompanying ottoman as if objects had a language that could be translated. But instead I found, behind the shadowy corner of the couch, a small spider that hovered over an intricate, nearly transparent web. Using a half-chewed pencil I discovered the addictive pleasure of destroying that web, and while I rubbed to nothing the thin, vaguely sticky threads that clung to my fingers, I watched the spider slowly, carefully rebuild.

I remember when I was eight years old the phone calls late at night, the hushed visits of Mother's relatives and her vacillating, tearful refusals during conversations behind closed doors. I soon learned it had been decided—without consulting me—that at the beginning of the summer I would visit my father and Paul for two weeks, and at the summer's end Paul would visit us. Though there were complications and delays, letters were exchanged and finally, during dinner one night, Mother spoke directly to Father over the phone to make the final arrangements. She began to talk with a twisted frown that then, defying gravity, slowly lifted into what might be called a smile. I realized that she was speaking to Paul. I didn't like the warm tones of her voice, or how her hands seemed to caress the receiver, so I began to choke on a piece of my potpie and she had to cut short the conversation, her glasses on as she slapped the back of her single son.

My mother said good-bye to me at the airport with a studied casualness, and I clung to her longer than was necessary. Then I walked down the narrow hallway to the plane. I had never flown before, yet I was barely amazed at the swift climb of the plane that dwarfed the houses and towns below, or at the otherworldly landscape of the clouds as we flew above them. All of my attention was on my approaching destination, and I felt the plane was speeding forward by the pull of the mysterious other half of my family.

When the plane landed, I walked down the ramp with the rest of the passengers, not quite sure where I was to meet my father and brother. I entered the large, domed airport building and there seemed to be people everywhere. Then I felt a touch on my shoulder and I turned to see myself, in different clothes.

"Mark? I'm Paul," my brother said.

He was just as overweight as I, the shirt above his belt bulging with baby rolls of flesh. Though I'd always known I had a twin, I had never fully imagined someone who looked *exactly* like me. He stood there, stiff and quiet, and somehow I knew he was thinking the same thing. I wanted to extend a hand, but the thought that his hand reaching to receive it would be the same in every detail stopped me. It would be like touching the cold surface of a mirror, and I was afraid. "Dad's waiting," Paul finally said, with my voice.

We walked together through the crowds and tried not to look at each other, embarrassed by the frightening attraction of our complete resemblance. A man in a shapeless gray jacket approached us cautiously, his roundish face somehow familiar. "Dad," I ventured, and I stood there. Could this ordinary-looking man be the horrible creature who had left my mother? "Son," he replied, but he looked back and forth nervously at Paul and me. I thought he might have forgotten what Paul had worn that morning and he wasn't sure which of us was his new son. "Thanks for inviting me," I said, and he smiled and strode forward. He crouched down and I let him embrace me. Paul stared at us and I stared back at him, my chin on my father's shoulder. Then Paul began to cough violently and Father released me to pat my brother's back. Yes, I then realized, this was a mirror that knew my own tricks.

We walked together to the baggage wheel and waited stiffly for my two small suitcases to appear. I looked at my father: he could have been anyone at the airport, though I didn't quite trust his harmless exterior. Then I noticed with fear that his hands were twitching in his pockets, but how could I have understood then the subtle movements of guilt and remorse? When the suitcases arrived we walked to the car and Father talked about all the plans he had for the coming weeks. I nodded my head, pretending interest, but I kept glancing at Paul. He was more than a mirror, I decided, unsettled, for mirrors have no voices, no independent movements; mirrors you can leave and your image disappears, but Paul walked along beside me, rubbing the edge of his nose with a fist—my own habitual gesture.

Father could sense my distraction, and when he put my bags away in the car trunk he almost closed the lid on his finger. "Damn!" he shouted, and he smacked the trunk with his other hand. Here my real father connected with my imagined one: he was the sort of man who beat objects if they didn't do what he wanted, and he might mistake me for a broken chair or a stuck window. As we drove along and I tried to answer Father's questions about my school and my grades—subjects about which I cared absolutely nothing—I thought that his ordinary hands around the steering wheel might secretly be waiting to strike me, or perhaps he would suddenly play chicken with an oncoming truck, not turning away until both of us begged him to stop in our identical voices. I fastened my seat belt and looked out at the midwestern landscape we traveled through: I had never seen anything so flat, and the enormous sky seemed to press down upon us.

Soon we drove into a town and stopped before a large, white, shingled house. "We're home," Father said. When we entered I stared avidly, for I knew that half of everything inside had been transplanted from my own house, and I hoped to finally see the invisible connections between what had been removed and what remained. Yet Father's own replacements were as cleanly matched as Mother's, and no discordant styles could serve as fault lines exposing the initial upheaval. Father saw my carefully directed curiosity and his hands twisted anxiously again in his pockets. He finally led us to Paul's room, where the walls were lined with shelves of expensive toy soldiers, and there was a second bed—the fold-up kind—in a corner.

"You'll be staying here, Mark," Father said. "Best way for two boys to get to know each other is to share a room." Paul and I looked at each other warily, uncertain that we wanted to be left alone.

"Well," Father continued, confused by our silence, "it's a bit late. I'll go fix us some dinner. You two play, or something." Father left, and I sat on the edge of my temporary bed, fiddling with the handle of one of my suitcases.

"Would you like to look at my soldiers?" Paul asked.

"Yeah," I answered, and as he led me through the room I discovered that he had toy figures for every imaginable conflict, some I'd barely heard of: the French and Indian Wars, the Boxer Rebellion, even something called the

Russo-Japanese War. I stared at his soldiers greedily: many had movable arms and heads, even detachable weapons, while others were metal, their details intricately painted. My own were generic plastic things, and I had only two kinds: the good guys and the bad guys. Paul talked me into playing with his knights for the War of the Roses, but I agreed only reluctantly, because I didn't know who had won and I was afraid he was giving me the knights for the losing side.

And so we played, but soon with little enjoyment, for we discovered we were evenly matched. My flank attack of cavalry from behind the night table was warned off by his archers, and his frontal offensive across the rug was checked by a pincer movement of my best troops. We even anticipated each other's anticipations, we plotted so much alike, and all our machinations proved as futile as trying to hide a secret from oneself. "*Move*, Val; attack, Roland," Paul whispered to his soldiers, foiling my sneak attack. As I hadn't been formally introduced to my knights, I silently led a retreat that was actually a trap, but Paul didn't allow his troops to follow. It was with relief that we heard Father call us to dinner.

"Have a good time, you two fellas?" he asked, serving us.

"Yeah," I replied without much energy. Paul remained silent, his mouth full, and when I looked at him I could see myself eating. While I chewed my way through combined mouthfuls of pork, potatoes, and succotash I watched Paul's own bloated cheeks; as I licked the last traces of sauce off each forkful I looked to see Paul's lips pucker around the tines. He caught my gaze and, as if a mirror could have opinions and make a face at what it saw, scowled at me, his lips moist with salad dressing. I was suddenly ashamed of my appetite and my small, overweight body. I wanted to lose pound after pound, collapse into another self, and then leave the strong pull of Paul's image behind. I began to eat slowly, and from each portion I pushed aside a bit that I wouldn't let myself touch. But to my despair, I saw that Paul also ate sparingly, and I understood his intentions were the same as my own. We continued to pick at our food until Father said, "You're both not very hungry, are you?"

"Not really," Paul managed to answer, and I nodded.

"Well, then how about dessert?" Father asked nervously as he took our plates to the sink. He walked to the refrigerator and returned with the desserts.

"Yumi-Creems," he announced, "Paul's favorite. I hope you like it, Mark."

The huge, delicious, eclairlike thing was my favorite too, but as I looked at the spacious mirror of my brother I knew I couldn't eat it. Instead, I tried to think of every disgusting, unsanitary process that might have gone into its making: the dirty hands that had probably rolled the pastry; the caked fingernails that must have slipped into the dough, leaving dark smudges that would later be covered by the chocolate frosting. But I was hungry, and the Yumi-Creem was warming on my plate. What if it *was* streaked with secret dirt? I thought. Yet as I lifted it to my lips I made myself see huge, crusted, fly-ridden vats of chocolate that hadn't been cleaned for days, and that was when I let my dessert slip to the kitchen floor.

"You *dropped* it," Paul said.

"It *fell*," I replied.

I looked down at the pastry on the floor. It was still salvageable. So when I shifted my chair to reach down and pick it up, I let one of the legs land right on it, smearing the dessert across the clean linoleum tiles.

Father grabbed some paper towels and we cleaned up

the mess together. "I'm sorry," I said, still not sure of him and afraid he might suddenly hit me. "It's all right, it's all right," he kept repeating. When we returned to the table I saw half a Yumi-Creem lying on my plate, the other half on Paul's.

"You can share mine," Paul said, smiling.

"That's okay, I'm not hungry." I pushed away from the table.

"Funny, I'm not either," Paul said, and he rose too. Father watched us, perplexed.

After washing the dishes we all walked to the living room and watched the television silently, as though we'd known each other for years and we hadn't a thing to say. When the closing credits rose on the screen for yet another situation comedy, Father said with exaggerated enthusiasm, "Hey, tomorrow's going to be a big day. You boys should be getting to bed."

"Okay," Paul said, and he kissed Father on the cheek. I realized I should do the same. My father's hands rose to embrace me when I kissed him, but I pulled away slightly from the strange sensation of beard stubble against my lips, and his arms then returned to the sides of his chair. I looked away and said good night.

While Paul made toothbrush noises in the bathroom, I stood in my pajamas before his small dresser mirror, comb in hand. I made threatening gestures at my image, pretending it was my brother, but it simply made threatening gestures back at me. Then I slowly, carefully parted my hair on the other side so I would look different from Paul. But when he returned from the bathroom I saw that he had moved *his* part. Paul stared at me glumly. There was no escape: we were still identical. Resigned, but also secretly impressed, we got into bed without a word and Paul turned out the light.

We lay in the dark, listening to each other's breathing for a long time. Finally, Paul asked, "What's she like?"

I didn't know how to answer. I could have said of Mother, "She cooks; she washes things," but that was all wrong. I could have mentioned her job, but I'd never really listened when she discussed it. I was too young to be able to detail her nervous laughter or the cautious gestures of her hands through her hair, and so, frustrated, I simply said, "She's great."

Paul remained quiet, and I was sure he was measuring his imagined mother against my inadequate description. Had he invented someone as forbidding as the father I'd visualized? "What's *Dad* really like?" I asked, hoping to interrupt Paul's thoughts.

Silence. He was having the same difficulties I'd had. Then he replied, "You saw. He's great, just great."

Surprising myself, I said, with terrible calmness, "That's not what I heard."

"Oh? *Who* says so?"

"Mom," I lied, and then, frightened, I found myself voicing my most secret suspicions about Father. "He used to put acid in her nail polish."

"Yeah?" Paul responded after some hesitation, his words clipped with contained anger, "*She* put Drano in his shaving cup."

I couldn't see my quiet, distracted mother plotting so destructively. Furious, I replied, "*He* put broken glass in her purse." I thought that soon we might be grappling blindly in the middle of the room.

"*She* threw a radio right at his head," Paul returned. My mother, however, was devoted to easy listening stations, and I could only imagine a sentimental melody hurtling toward Father's ear.

"*He* cut all of her dresses in half with a scissors."

"*She* set fire to Dad's newspaper while he was reading it," Paul almost spit back. But I was suddenly silent, for I knew Mother was afraid of any sort of flame. When she cooked she even had me light the gas burners, dangling a potholder before my face for protection. Paul was lying, just as I was, and then I understood that in our separate isolations we had shared the same private fears. I said, halfheartedly, "He slammed the silverware drawer . . . on her fingers."

I waited a long time for Paul's reply, not sure if my twin had heard the doubt in my voice and was experiencing his own. Finally he offered, without passion, "She glued his briefcase shut." At that moment our vicious, invented parents began to dissolve in the darkness.

"He put flies in her mashed potatoes," I said cautiously.

"She put a frog in his pillow," Paul replied, a silly accusation.

"He put her address book in the toaster," I said, and then added, "Poof!"

We both giggled. Relieved, we continued to confess our childish images of what could make a marriage go wrong.

"He put her parakeet in the dryer!" I said loudly, imagining a squawking, circling thing.

"She put toilet water in his Tang!" Paul whooped.

In my innocence I offered, with a shout, "He peeked at her when she was undressing!"

"She hid his underpants!" Paul howled, thumping his bed.

"He barfed on her shoes!" I hooted, gagging for dramatic emphasis, and we shared great snorts of laughter.

We heard heavy footsteps. "Hey, who's making all that noise in there?" Father shouted, though with an edge of satisfaction in his voice. We lay as quietly as we could, suppressing our giggles as he growled, with obvious pleasure, "Some boys may not know that it's way past the time for fooling around!" We were silent, and somewhere down the block a door shut and a car started up. Then we heard Father's confident footsteps return down the hallway. He didn't know that he was now outnumbered.

We were exhilarated by our conspiracy of silence during Father's chastisement, but we remained quiet, and I thought of how the next day we could do and say everything in unison around Father, pretending to be as surprised by this as he was. I shifted under the covers and Paul did too, as our stomachs began to slowly rumble and gurgle. Already we were anxious for the morning's breakfast. Our movements echoed each other's when we turned our pillows over, when we rubbed itchy ankles against the mattresses. As I listened I imagined that we were interchangeable: when it was time for me to leave, *Paul* could return, having been coached in whatever small quirks of mine weren't identical to his own, and I could stay; and at the end of the summer I would visit, pretending to be Paul, pretending I was seeing Mother for the first time. Somewhere outside an unfamiliar, dull metal noise repeated itself, and I had the unaccustomed pleasure of knowing that my twin was sharing the same frightening dark. Paul yawned, I yawned, and we slowly adjusted our breathing to each other—inhale, silence, exhale, silence—as we drifted together into sleep.

Stan and Patty

It's early Saturday morning and Stan and Patty are abruptly awakened by the sirens: another hill in town has collapsed overnight. Concerned as Stan and Patty are, they dress slowly and, as always, they dress each other, like last night's seduction in reverse: his hands button her skirt; hers fasten his belt. They finish in the usual way, each helping the other tie the laces of the last shoe. Then Stan stares out the bedroom window at Knob Hill, his favorite. It collapsed weeks ago. There it lies in a puddle of its own wrinkles while children play among the furrows. Filled with the sight, Stan is unable to move, and it seems to Patty that he is as sunken as that hill. She holds his hand and tickles the palm with her nails. Stan comes out of it, and just in time too, because the threads in the seams of his shirt are beginning to unravel.

The sirens continue in the distance. Walking past their strangely warped furniture, Stan and Patty decide to skip breakfast and they join the crowds outside. The town is a flatland. No matter that the streets are numbered, people everywhere are confused and lost from the lack of landmarks. Even the birds overhead circle where the hills once were, vainly trying to land on an invisible curve of air. Stan and Patty head for the flashing red lights down the street.

Soon they stand among the crowd of townspeople surrounding the former hill. While the police and fire departments confer together, the locals argue. They are divided into two camps: those who had lived on the hill and their neighbors who had not. Those who had lived on the hill complain bitterly of the loss—though fearfully anticipated—of their beautiful view, and they propose that scaffolds be built at the town's expense and their new homes be placed at the top. Those who hadn't lived on the hill, feeling newly possessed of a relatively lovely view now that the hill is no longer there to obstruct it, oppose this idea.

Stan and Patty watch in silence, apart from the others. For them, it has always been this way. Before they met, at parties Patty was the pause in the conversation; at home Stan was the wrong number. He had carried this trait into his work: as a telephone repairman, Stan's specialties were dial tones and busy signals. Patty, for her part, had often been mistaken for a mannequin at the department store where she worked.

As the voices of the townspeople rise, Stan and Patty decide to leave. They walk down the sidewalk, hand in hand, and it buckles behind them, the cracks in the cement like the intertwining of fingers. Passersby, rushing to join the angry crowd, don't notice.

Stan and Patty head for her favorite hill, which she visits every day as if she were a bouquet of flowers presented to its flat grave. There it is, no longer reflected in the park's lake; instead, Chester Hill's leveled edges reach just past the shoreline and rock with the gentle lapping of the waves. She goes out as far as she safely can. Then, complete silence except for the sighs of disappointed Patty and the stones she throws into the water. Stan waits a few minutes and then leads Patty by the hand to the edge of the woods in the park. They sit and hold each other beneath a tree. It begins to smolder. Leaves turn brilliant red and then brown, and then fall from the branches, even though it's spring. Stan and Patty, eyes closed, don't notice, though the rustling of the dry leaves on the ground makes them restless. They walk off, while behind them birds' nests burst into flame.

Stan and Patty, strolling down the quiet streets, play their favorite, private game. He makes dialing motions in the air and she moves as if to answer the silent ringing. Oh oh, wrong number. But how could Patty pretend this while Stan's sad eyes say it isn't true? Stan and Patty, both so lonely for so long, can't keep their eyes off of each other, even when crossing the street. Instead, they're almost run over by the fire engines that are racing toward the park. Stan and Patty stop and stare and then continue on their way.

There is a noisy crowd down the road. As Stan and Patty approach they see it's a number of angry shopkeepers arguing in front of their stores, arguing over who will repair their common sidewalk, the cement now buckled up in different directions. All the shopkeepers use chalk and string to measure their responsibility, a responsibility, it seems, that is always smaller than their neighbors'.

Stan and Patty watch in silence, sorry for the owners and their anger. Patty especially stands very still. Stan is reminded of when they first met. He was repairing a cashier's phone at a local department store and placed a roll of cable on Patty's arm, thinking she was part of a display. In surprise she gave a little shout and he turned to her. Their eyes met, and for Stan it was the clearing of a bad connection. Now they're inseparable. They even have their own shop: Patty sells designer telephone seconds and Stan repairs them.

The shopkeepers continue to argue. The butcher and shoe repairman, red-faced from shouting, shake pieces of chalk at each other. Stan and Patty, saddened, continue along their favorite route through the town. They walk past the elementary school with its melted monkey-bars, the restaurant closed for repairs, and the abandoned lot that recently was a drive-in theater. Already, vines are growing up the speaker stands.

Stan and Patty stop for a moment of nostalgia: this was where they had their first date. They were nervous through the coming attractions. Stan brought to Patty's attention the points of interest on the dashboard and she agreed that the built-in cigarette lighter was quite lovely. Then they both looked out the windows and hoped aloud that it wouldn't rain. But a random touching of hands over popcorn unleashed Stan and Patty on each other. For Patty, all those years of surreptitious high school crushes, of frozen longing, erupted at their lips, could not be contained in the brushing of their eyelashes. Stan felt the same. It was as if the memory of all his threading of underground phone lines blended into the ringing of one gigantic, ecstatic phone call that jammed the lines of every other home in town. Stan's old car then settled softly in its frame, while projected on the screen across the lot was not the scheduled film but a kind of smoldering light show, broken only by vague glimpses of groping hands and homely, kissing faces. Stan and Patty didn't share the audience's alarm—they were too wrapped up in themselves, the cigarette lighter all the while glowing in the dark. At the end of the evening's feature they were the first to leave. None of the other cars would start: the battery fluid in every one had evaporated. Stan and Patty drove off, oblivious to the distant cries of customer outrage.

Now, while two dogs chase each other around the old concession stand, Stan and Patty hold hands and sigh beneath the weather-worn screen. Then they walk down the street to the corner and wait for the bus. The traffic light beside them blinks green, then yellow, and red. Stan and Patty rub the sides of their knees together while they turn their heads in the direction of the approaching bus. The light stutters yellow twice, red three times quickly, and one long green on all sides. The intersection fills with uncertain motorists, scraping each other's fenders, as Stan and Patty board the newly arrived bus. The driver slowly makes his way through the congested street. Stan and Patty hold hands, and through the thin fabric of shirt and blouse their shoulders press together. It's warm inside and passengers begin to open the windows. With newspapers they fan the steam that seems to be rising from the cushioned seats. When the metal screws that hold the colorful advertisements in place on the walls begin to hiss and glow, everyone rushes from the bus, shoes smoking from the shining hot aisle. Stan and Patty leave too, arm in arm, thinking they've come to the end of the line. They walk down the street, unaware of the traffic stopped for blocks because of a bus that's fused to the middle of the road by its melted tires.

The sun sets and Stan and Patty are almost home. They make their way past wilted front-lawn flower beds, cindered picket fences, and, beneath the distorted glare of a twisted streetlamp, an insistently ringing phone in an open, empty booth. Stan stops before it, his hands twitching at the sound, but Patty gently tugs at his arm and they turn the corner for home. They walk in the front door, into the rooms filled with warped and unmanageable furniture. Lamps are leaning against walls, tables and chairs are tilted at conflicting angles, and rugs are curled up like thin paper. As always, Stan and Patty don't notice anything but each other.

They make dinner together. Patty prepares the main dish and Stan slices vegetables for the salad. Every clank of pot and clink of spoon that Patty makes, Stan turns and watches. Every whish of knife through mushroom or tomato that Stan makes, Patty watches too. Each time they turn they move closer together, their own private telephone line. They embrace. On the stove their soup comes to a boil, even though Patty forgot to turn the burner on.

Stan and Patty eat slowly, each mouthful of chicken and sweet pepper a mime of kisses. But the best thing about dinner is its ending, for with the dishes washed, Stan and Patty quickly leave the kitchen. They walk past the living room, where in the corner the television suddenly blinks on and switches channels as rapidly as a hand running across a tingling, naked back. They walk down the hall where pictures sway against the walls like the motion of legs searching for a tender cove. Once in the bedroom, Stan and Patty undress one another: their clothes fall to the floor in a conspiracy of bare skin and fingers, and the carpet crinkles under their curled toes. Around them, the night table lamp shudders, the closet door hinges bend and hum, and the curtains twist up along the edge of the window. Stan and Patty lead each other to the bed and to the evening's inevitable, surprise-laden, and delicious lovemaking—as inevitable, in fact, as the announcement tomorrow morning that another hill in town has collapsed overnight.

The Kite

The weekend ahead of them, Daniel and Margaret were window-shopping after work and they were anxious to give themselves a little gift. Hands held absently, they walked from one store to another, ignoring the threatening clouds, and then they stopped before a candy shop window. The glass front reflected their impassive faces as they peered in at the sweets arranged in the shapes of flowers: the fat bulb of a licorice tulip, an elaborate caramel orchid, and the overlapping petals of a chocolate rose. "Yum," Daniel said, "I'm hungry."

Margaret poked his stomach. "You're always hungry."

"Who, me?" he replied, suddenly smiling. He puffed out his cheeks as if he were a fat man, and Margaret led him away.

It started to rain in thick, heavy drops, and Daniel and Margaret ran to the next store and entered. It was filled with kites. Uncomfortable being in a children's store, they looked back at the instant streams that poured along the sidewalk outside before they finally walked slowly through the aisles. Kites were hanging everywhere above the shelves, absolutely still, as if caught in the air. They were in the shapes of cobras, stingrays, bats, and hornets. Others featured astronauts and samurai. At one display, kites filled with the faces of baseball stars together formed the diamond shape of an infield, and in its center was a kite with the printed figure of a pitcher in the middle of his windup.

Then they saw the large, tubular goldfish kite, suspended from the ceiling in a corner, and its bulbous eyes met their own in a friendly stare. They could easily see its pink fins streaking through a blue sky that could also be a blue ocean, every flutter of paper fins a reaction to an unseen ripple of wind or current. Margaret felt an urge to touch it, yet she was relieved that it was beyond the reach of her outstretched hand. "Let's buy it," Daniel said. They stared up at it quietly. They couldn't remember when either of them had last flown a kite, but they wanted to fly this one. It was sold as a kit, and though they were disappointed when the saleswoman opened the thin cardboard box and they could only see one section of its folded-up face, they had her wrap it, along with a roll of string. Then they ran to their car in the last light fall of the rain, the kite under Daniel's jacket.

In the car, Daniel swiftly shook his damp hair. "Down, Fido," Margaret said. He growled. She patted his head and he began to breathe through his open mouth, his tongue out. "Good boy," she said. They drove off, the covered kite lying on the backseat, and they both continued to pretend that it wasn't a year since the death of their daughter.

That night Margaret raided the ragbag in the closet and cut thin, colored strips of cloth for the kite's tail. Beside her Daniel bent the balsa spars into place and carefully glued the delicate paper until the kite became a goldfish, identical to the one they'd seen displayed. He felt an immense affection for it and restrained himself from lightly spreading his hand across its smooth surface. Then he poked it in the nose and it shivered. "We're gonna have some fun tomorrow, huh?" he asked. Margaret nodded and attached the tail to the back fins. She picked up the kite and laid it along the length of the coffee table, where it displaced the *TV Guide* and a smiling, ceramic Buddha, his fat arms stretched wide. She hoped there would be a clear sky the next day.

"What's on tonight?" Daniel asked. Remembering how their daughter used to flip wildly past the channels, he turned the dial as slowly as he could, past puppets singing in ordered rows; past a serious-faced, aging anchorman; then past a flashing game board and hopping contestants. Finally they chose a comedy about waitresses attempting to fill short orders in a restaurant whose newly waxed floor was incredibly slippery. Margaret sat down on the couch beside Daniel, and while they watched, she could imagine their daughter's sharp, high laughter. When the show was over, Daniel grabbed a leg and tickled Margaret's bare foot. She tried to tickle back, her hands skirting around his waist, but soon she gave in to his fingers and wriggled helplessly. Finally she kicked his grip loose and ran laughing from the couch. She escaped down the hall and Daniel chased her into the bedroom, where she hid in the dark. He closed the door behind him and listened for her breathing, listened for any small movement.

Huge clouds rolled overhead in the morning, but by the afternoon the sky slowly began to clear and Daniel and Margaret took their kite to the park. They had hoped to watch other people flying kites first before letting loose their own, but on such a day almost no one was there. They walked to an area free of trees and Daniel unraveled a length of string. He attached it under the open mouth of the kite while Margaret held its pink, paper scales with her hands. Daniel let out more string and started dragging it along. Margaret watched her feet as she followed, careful not to step on the cloth tail rippling on the grass. The kite shuddered as the wind ran through it, and it began to lift. "It's in the air!" Margaret shouted, and Daniel ran without looking back, feeling the line taut behind him. Then he turned around and there it was, a floating goldfish. Its movements seemed stiff, jerky, as if unaccustomed to this new life. Then Margaret took over the string and easily directed the sailing kite, slowly letting out line and drawing it back in. They took turns, improving as they made a circuit around the park.

The kite cast a shadow that swept across the field and Margaret playfully chased after it. Daniel quickly understood her game and teasingly guided the kite, curving its shadow away from her just as she was about to step into its shade. "Hey!" she complained, laughing, as Daniel sped the shadow far from her, but then it stopped and turned, rushing back toward her, and now she was being chased. Margaret ran away quickly, but soon the swift, dark patch spread over her and continued on. She slowed down, breathing hard, as she watched it shrink in the distance.

When it was Margaret's turn she made a few sharp swoops at Daniel as he ambled along, but then, as if the wind had vanished, there was a sudden droop of string and the kite began to fall. It was so unexpected that Daniel had to run as it plunged above him. It's a fish, he thought as he watched, and it's only diving deeper into the water. But soon it was a shattered kite, with a twisted spar that arched through its broken head, the large round eyes staring crazily. The pink, delicate scales of its torn fins fluttered against the ground. It did look like a fish, but one that was dying for water and gasping its final breaths on the park grass. They stood above it. Daniel bent down and twirled the tip of a ripped fin around his fingers and said, "Maybe we could patch it up."

"Maybe," Margaret replied, and she gathered up the kite.

Back home, Margaret carefully put the kite in a corner of the living room, between the ornamental fireplace and a plant stand overflowing with a lush vine. As Daniel met its impossibly wide-eyed gaze, he thought it looked like a mythological beast: a fish able to fly, but now wounded and crawling on dry land. Suddenly he heard it hiss like a reptile, but then he realized it was the bubbling of oil in the kitchen where Margaret was beginning dinner.

Daniel and Margaret watched television without pleasure that evening. While idly passing sections of the newspaper to each other, they sat through a documentary on plant life and a televised opera, anything their daughter wouldn't have wanted to watch with them. But finally they switched to a situation comedy: the studio audience was laughing loudly and often as two people secretly crawled and stalked about in the same room for an unmailed, hidden letter, each of them always just out of the other's peripheral vision. Margaret didn't want to see the end and said she was tired, but Daniel couldn't stop watching and said he would soon follow. He stood before the television as he listened to Margaret prepare for bed. The two people continued their search, but they only discovered each other in a confusion of arms and legs as they abruptly bumped together and the audience howled. Daniel turned off the set and the lights and let his eyes grow accustomed to the dark before walking down the hall. At the bedroom entrance he watched Margaret's restless figure under the covers. She was asleep, he could tell, but her body was slightly, slowly moving, as if she were traveling somewhere in the night. He lay down beside her.

After his own restlessness, Daniel fell asleep and dreamt that the living room was filled with salty waves and he was swimming, splashing water against the wallpaper and the closed windows. He lay on his back and floated, staring at the ceiling: its white, rough plaster surface became a full sky of clouds. He heard a splash and realized he wasn't alone in the room: someone was underwater. He dove down, breath held and eyes bulging as he swam under tables and chairs that seemed to be anchored to the floor, but he found no one. He started to rise for air and then he saw above him a small body floating face down, the tiny face obscured as his rising air bubbles broke against it.

Margaret opened her eyes in the dark, awakened by Daniel stirring beside her. She turned to him and he slowly quieted. She hesitated, then lifted her hand and stroked his hair. It felt rough, like dry grass. She touched his cheek but Daniel stirred again, away from her. Margaret lay quiet, the tips of her fingers still aware of his face as she returned to sleep, and while she slept Daniel's body slowly moved back to her.

Margaret dreamt she was their kite, miraculously repaired. She was flying, connected by a thin line to someone far away on the distant ground. Her tail of bright crepe twirled in the wind, above the tops of a huge expanse of trees. Their uppermost branches waved, as if beckoning her to return, but she rose higher until she was in a white haze of cloud. Its brightness confused her and then she realized she was falling: the ground swiftly swelled up below her and erased the sky. Then she was alone in a field surrounded by trees, her balsa frame shattered. From the trees appeared a young girl with straight red hair who walked, hand outstretched, toward Margaret's twisting tail of crepe. But it slipped away from the eager fingers, slipped away with the same wind that had lifted Margaret to the sky and then brought her crashing down to this lonely spot. Margaret was alone again. The distant trees snapped their branches together.

When she woke in the morning, staring at the ceiling, Margaret felt at first that she was still lying broken on the grass, the clouds above her. She closed her eyes, trying to recapture the dream, but it faded when she heard Daniel sit up beside her. He felt he had just come up for air and he glanced around, slowly recognizing the room. Daniel looked down at his wife, thinking she was asleep. He could see their child in her face and he felt as though he and Margaret were once again kneeling over their daughter at the beach, surrounded by a silent, nervous crowd, the gulls sweeping overhead. He dressed and walked down the hall to the kitchen to prepare breakfast.

Daniel had already sliced fat from the bacon and had the bread out to toast when he heard Margaret in the living room. He put down the spatula, stood in the doorway, and watched her walk to the corner where the kite lay huddled. She was bent over it, looking into the huge eyes, her fingernails scratching against the painted pupils. "Good morning," he said, and she quickly turned around, surprised.

"Sorry," he murmured. They looked at each other, unsure of what to say next.

"I'll go get the Sunday paper," Margaret finally said. She stood up. "Do you want to come along?"

"Well, I was just starting breakfast."

"That's okay, we'll only be a few minutes."

It was windy outside, the sky a clear, clean blue as they walked the four blocks to the stationery store. While Daniel bought the paper, Margaret stared down the long, empty aisles of colored notebooks, greeting cards, magazines, and comic books. The register rang and they left. Daniel held the newspaper before him, the ends of the pages lightly snapping from the wind, and together they read the disturbing headlines. All the economic indicators were down. Unemployment was up. A tornado had churned through the center of a town in the Midwest and swept it all away. Margaret shuddered and imagined standing in a leveled house that looked like a pile of broken twigs. Where had everything inside gone? Then she saw herself and Daniel torn into the air, the ground below a wide and spinning circle, both of them flailing among flying doors and tables.

Daniel stopped. She looked up and saw that he had led them not home but by the park. Across from them was a stretch of trees, and rising behind them in the air were three kites. Though the trees prevented Daniel and Margaret from seeing the children who guided the long, invisible lines of string, they could hear their high, nervous shouts. Daniel could imagine the children's movements from the loops and curves of the kites. One must be standing alone, giving the wind its way, while the other two must be running together, pulling the kites behind them. But he couldn't be sure; he only guessed. Margaret watched the kites spurt higher and she somehow wanted them to break free from their strings and soar away. But then the unseen children began tugging in the kites. They swooped lower and lower, sometimes so close to each other they almost touched and entangled their brightly colored tails. Margaret didn't want to watch them disappear behind the trees.

She took a step off the curb. One of the kites dove to just above the tops of the trees and then rose again, slightly. The others followed. She would soon lose sight of them. Margaret began to walk across the street. A car swerved and honked as it passed her. "Margaret, wait!" Daniel shouted, for she was starting to run, staring at the sky. He glanced up at the kites looping lower, and then he began to chase her. She didn't look back as he gained on her, and he didn't call out again. She dashed across a short stretch of lawn and entered the line of trees. Daniel was right behind, but when he reached her side she didn't stop. Margaret glanced at him, her mouth open and contorted from her breathing. They both remained quiet and Daniel found himself pacing her. They raced together through the trees, separating to avoid a thicket of brush, leaping over logs, and then they ran into the clearing, toward the startled children.

Cave Drawings

Maryanne met him at her uncle's wake. She was eighteen. He looked older and that was all right with her. He was, like the dead man, a member of the Optimists' Club and had helped organize the Punt, Pass, and Kick Competition, which was why he was here paying his respects. At least that was what Maryanne imagined about him as she stood with her back to the open casket and watched his polite and nervous mingling. And though he was taking much too long to get to her she patiently waited and tried to decide what his name might be. Cal? Bobby? Jeff?

"Hello, I'm Jim," he said while he stood beside her and, Of course, she thought, look at that brown hair; his name couldn't be anything else. "I'm not related, but Mr. Marshall was my supervisor and I'm sorry what happened," he said, but she barely listened, watching instead the circles and ovals his two lips made when he spoke. Only after he repeated his question did she reply, "Oh, I'm a niece. I work the register at Kwik Shop and I crochet pocketbooks and plant holders on the side. What do you do?" And then he began to make those pretty shapes with his mouth again, saying he worked nights driving the street sweeper, that it was quiet work, almost relaxing, and then that awful Aunt Pam interrupted him and asked would he like to meet the widow? Maryanne stood with her back to the open casket and watched Jim idly shake hands with more people he didn't know until he left. Her mother waved to her but Maryanne pretended not to see and looked away. No, she wasn't going to sit in a corner and mind the stray children. Instead, she walked through the crowd of family and, surrounded by flowers, knelt beside the corpse without looking at it and whispered, "Thank you, Uncle Ted, for bringing Jim here tonight. I hope you go to heaven. Amen."

The week after the funeral Maryanne stood behind the counter at Kwik Shop and waited. It rained twice. People came in and bought newspapers, potato chips, and lighter fluid. They used the pay phone. Teenage boys stared at the covers of girlie magazines wrapped in plastic. When the store was empty, Maryanne sketched new designs for plant holders and imagined just how the yarn would cling to a clay pot overflowing with leaves. If someone came in and asked for a Slush Cup, she worked the crushed-ice machine and looked out the plate glass window at the street. Beside her the hot dogs on their rack circled as in a Ferris wheel, sizzling in their skins.

Maryanne borrowed her mother's car that Friday and drove into town with Sally, her best friend. They went into a bar and sipped on beers while boys sat next to them and talked and tried to buy them more. Sally danced with one of them but Maryanne just sat on her barstool, looked at her face in the mirror, and replied to all offers that her feet hurt. When it was way past twelve Sally stopped dancing and giggled softly to Maryanne that her partner would drive her home but not, she hoped, too quickly. Maryanne said fine and have fun. By two o'clock she finished sipping her second beer and she left alone.

She drove through the streets of the town, not lost but not going anywhere, either. A few times she stopped, listened, and then drove on again. Finally, idling before a stop sign, she heard a distant rumble. It grew until she saw the street sweeper. It looked like the huge head of a catfish, its whiskers twirling and scouring the intersection that it crossed three blocks away. Maryanne turned her headlights off and followed, down streets lit with moon between the shadows of the trees. She drove slowly after him, a hundred yards behind, her mother's car hugging the sidewalks as he did. She even lumbered in a curve, just as he did in the distance, around cars their owners had forgotten to park on side streets. What if it wasn't him, she thought, what if there were *two* sweepers and she was following the wrong one? Maryanne turned on the radio. A man sang about a friend he'd lost and why. A man and a woman sang together about a fire only the two of them had. Then a woman sang about her sad eyes and all the other parts of her face. Then the weather came on and Maryanne shut the radio off. She just followed the sweeper, and always before her were its two steady rear red lights. It made a slow U-turn in the street. Maryanne watched the heavy graceful curving until she realized, "Oh, he'll see me," and she pulled her car to the curb and parked before a dark house. The sweeper, and Jim's profile, drove past her. She sat in the car and listened until she couldn't hear the rumble any longer.

"I stopped off at Sally's and had coffee," she told her mother the next morning. Her mother didn't believe this but she hoped it was true. Maryanne pretended she was interested in something else, as she always did when she lied. While her mother stared at her she tried to read the local tourist brochure for Henry Pike Caverns, her favorite, that was stuck to a corner of the bulletin board. Henry Pike, it said, was an early settler and an Indian fighter. He discovered a cavern where a small tribe of Indians lived and he set a fire at the entrance. They all died of smoke inhalation. But their beautiful cave drawings still survive and are on display and open to the public 10 till 4. Maryanne had gone to see those drawings so often she could almost imagine them now.

The large pot of water came to a boil and her mother got up, took it off the burner, and put on another one. The steam rose in her kitchen, making a fine mist on the ceiling. It was twelve days since the water treatment plant in their small township had shut down for six weeks of repairs, after issuing warnings about invisible but dangerous bacteria. Her mother rubbed her hand against the clouded window and looked through the moist view of her fingerprints at the parked car in the gravel driveway. "How can you stand it in here?" Maryanne asked, waving her arms. "I can hardly breathe."

The next Friday, Maryanne didn't go to the bar. Instead, she entered a slow line of cars, paid her three-fifty, and turned into the lot of the drive-in for the five features of the Dusk-to-Dawn Weekend Special. She entered behind a pickup truck full of young men. There were three in the back, sitting on lawn chairs. The driver kept stopping short, trying to make them fall out of their seats. They laughed and held on to the sides of the truck and pounded at the back window filled with their friends' mocking faces. One of the boys turned and winked broadly at her, distorting his face. Maryanne drove a safe and slow distance behind them, and when they parked at a speaker stand she kept going until she came to the end of the lane.

After a few minutes a film appeared on the screen describing all the food and drinks available at the refreshment stand, but Maryanne wasn't going to leave the car. Finally, the first movie came on. Two people died during the opening credits and the actors' names appearing on the screen were splashed with red. It was a spy movie. Maryanne turned the sound off the speaker attached to her window, but even so she could hear the sound of the gunshots coming from the cars around her. The next movie was a comedy, but she only giggled uncertainly because, with her speaker now on again, she couldn't hear if the people in the other cars were laughing. She wished she'd bought popcorn, but she stayed in her car. She couldn't tell what the third movie was about. It might have been a love story because two people kept kissing, or it might have been a comedy because they were always interrupted. But when a car they were in drove off a cliff she decided it was another spy picture.

She looked at her watch. It was time to leave. She put the speaker back on its hook and drove out of the lot, heading downtown. She imagined, as she often did, that her mother was invisible beside her, watching and judging. But it was late, her mother would be asleep by now, and so Maryanne smiled and forgot about her.

She parked in front of a house with a FOR SALE sign on the lawn. A dog barked a few times and then it was quiet again. Soon she heard the far-off drone and she started her car and followed it. First she saw the twin red lights at the back of the sweeper. As she drew closer Maryanne could see the large turning brushes that rippled under the occasional light from the streetlamps. Again, she followed a hundred yards behind, and when the sweeper began to make a U-turn she was already parked and waiting for it to return and pass by. But she sat there frozen and watched instead as it slowed down and stopped in the middle of the street across from her. The window rolled down and

Jim's face appeared, a little afraid. He stared into the dark carefully, but when he saw her he began to smile.

"It's awfully lonely in this sweeper. Care for a ride?"

Oh, she thought in her embarrassment, what will I do? "Is it against regulations?" she heard herself ask.

"Who'll know? Only you and me are up this late."

She got out of her car and looked up and down the street to see if the windows were lit in any of the houses. Darkness everywhere. She walked over to the passenger side, climbed up, and sat down. He was still smiling. She looked away from him and stared at the shift as he started up the sweeper, and at the knobs and levers that changed the direction and speed of the large brushes as they drove down the street.

"Where's the radio in this thing?"

"Don't have a radio," he said, pleased she was making herself comfortable.

She hummed, imitating the drone of the engine, and it became a song, rising and falling, not a song she knew but something she made up.

"That sounds better than the radio," he said. He watched her face framed in the side window. Her lips, even after she stopped, were pressed together from her humming.

They were quiet for a few blocks. Maryanne looked out her window at the huge bristles of the turning brush. They seemed dangerous, unfriendly.

"Does this thing really *clean* the streets?"

"Well, it's more like a wash and rubdown."

The sweeper droned on for a few more blocks.

"Is this what you do, all night?"

"Sometimes I do tricks."

"Tricks?"

"Just wait."

They continued down the street, curving out around cars,

curving back against the curb. Maryanne looked behind them: just a faint red glare from the sweeper's rear lights. But far away she saw a clear circle of light from a street-lamp, and she realized how easily she'd been spotted.

Jim turned down a side street, then another, and there before them was a supermarket and its empty parking lot. Speeding up, Jim headed straight for it. He turned grace-fully into the entrance and the brushes swept a fat path across the painted parking lanes. Maryanne winced, imagining the lines filled with invisible cars. "Hold on," Jim said, smiling, and he veered sharply and locked the steering wheel so that they turned a mad circle around a parking lot lamppost, its light encompassing them. "Oh, do a figure eight," she shouted, surprised at herself, and the sweeper broke from the lamppost in a lazy curve as Jim said, "At your service."

Soon the parking lot was covered with huge brush strokes, wet patterns that crisscrossed and spiraled over the angles of the white parking lanes. Maryanne held on to the inside door handle and imagined herself in an utterly unpredictable carnival ride, all their spins and turns following no set track but made up as they went along. "Turn right!" she screamed. "No, left this time," he said, and with a flourish of the wheel they looped past the Dumpster. "Now right," she repeated and he twisted the sweeper where she pointed. They headed straight for the supermarket, the truck lights flaring against the glass front, growing larger. "Should I turn," Jim laughed, "should I turn?" "Oh, I don't care," she said slowly, her eyes closed from the glare. She felt the sweeper sharply veer and she opened her eyes to see a long, shin-ing, too close row of shopping carts. Jim spun the wheel again and they headed for the exit. Maryanne looked out the rear window at the lot. They were leaving behind a network of crazy wet trails, glistening in the lamplight, that were already beginning to dry and disappear and yet somehow seemed so familiar.

They turned onto a main street and Jim returned to work, keeping the brushes close to the edge of the sidewalk as they drove block after block. Maryanne's heart was still beating quickly and it seemed to her that the sweeper was moving too slowly. They rumbled along, the only sound in the quiet, darkened town. Only once, in all the rows of houses, did they see an open, lit window, and as they passed they saw the back of someone's head in a chair and the dull TV light of an old black-and-white movie. Maryanne and Jim didn't talk, as though they'd already said all they needed to.

Soon they were driving through the slow half-light of before dawn. What beautiful patterns they'd made in the parking lot, Maryanne thought as she tried to keep her eyes open at the confusing grid of streets. She'd only blink, it seemed, but when she opened her eyes they'd be on another block.

"I'm so tired."

"You need some coffee. My shift is almost over. If you like, we could go to the diner when I'm done."

"Eggs and juice would be fine too," she whispered.

"Good. I'll drop you off at your car and you can follow me to the garage. Where was it you parked?"

Maryanne sat up. "I forget. Oh, no, I wasn't watching the street signs. Did you notice?"

He didn't answer. "No," he then said quietly, "I was too busy watching you follow me."

Maryanne didn't deny it. The night was, after all, now a secret for both of them. "What are we going to do?" she asked.

"Well, I don't know." Jim smiled. "Go back over the

night's run, I guess." He turned the brushes off. There was no need for them now and this way he could drive faster. It was getting lighter. A car drove by.

"I'm speeding up here, so you just look out the window for that car of yours, okay?"

She stared as hard as she could so her tired eyes wouldn't shut. How could she now be lost in a town she'd lived outside of all her life? What would she tell her mother? She tried to remember where she'd left the car, and as Jim drove on she instead realized what she was reminded of by the paths they'd left in the parking lot. It was the first time she'd visited the local caverns. The guide had led Maryanne and her group through narrow paths cut into the rock. She'd felt as if she were in a movie and they were all escaping from a prison through a tunnel. Finally they had come to an open, domed space and they'd crowded together in the dim light provided by two small bulbs at the entrance. Then the guide had switched on the flood lamps and there before them on the shiny limestone walls were the Indian drawings. They were beautiful overlapping designs, geometric swirls whose different colors reflected the light, and they seemed to lead everywhere across the moist walls, like a map, like a maze she could just walk into and disappear in.

The Deserted House

When Nana sang in the shower we all listened in spite of ourselves. With her false teeth in a glass by the bathroom sink, her gums padded her beloved, ancient melodies beyond recognition. Father would sit in his chair downstairs and hum along, hidden by his newspaper. He was a good son and his harmony was meant to drown out Nana, but he was always defeated by her unpredictable phrasing. I would continue with whatever book I was holding and read the words slowly to those steps of uncertain melody, so that the story became a series of songs threatening to lurch off the page. My older brother hid, a hater of any sort of music. Mother made emphatic noises in the kitchen with half-open cabinet doors and idle pots or dishes. Reminded of her own father—a former *professional* musician, we were always told—Mother was soon beside Father in the living room, pleading that Grandad, a longtime widower, finally be allowed to visit. As usual, Father defended Nana's singing, pretending the argument was about music and not some unforgiven rift.

After one particularly faltering concert by Nana, Mother went into a protracted, unspecified mourning. For days she kept the curtains closed and all the houseplants shrouded. When sunlight finally returned to the rooms, erasing the recent hint of mildew, Father found he had agreed to a summer's stay for Grandad. At once Mother traveled to the West to help with preparations. Father stayed home, regretting his decision, while my older brother and I were filled with excitement: we had never met Grandad. The night before he was to arrive, Father rearranged the furniture in all the rooms, as if he didn't want Grandad to visit our house but a new one he had just made up.

My brother and I watched from a careful distance as he dragged armchairs across wide stretches of carpet, hauled bookshelves to different walls, pushed beds to opposite corners, and set lamps to light up new tables. Nana followed in Father's wake, sweeping away the dust shadows left on the rugs by the moved furniture. She worked so swiftly that she had to wait for Father to complete a new regrouping; sitting in a newly resettled chair she regarded with growing disbelief the changing face of each room. Nana, though small, was speedy. Whenever our parents were angry with my brother and me they had her catch us. Often when we saw her coming we stopped rather than run a futile race, for soon Nana would be at our sides, enveloping us in the smell of her dental plate paste. But we always forgave her because once she had us by the wrists she interceded for us and her pleadings, more often than not, caused our parents to relent.

The next day, gathered in the living room of our new, strange house, we waited for Mother and Grandad to arrive from the airport. "They can take the taxi home," Father had said, and Nana had clicked her tongue in disapproval. I sat on the couch, trying to read a book about a sad river that was lost in the ocean, hoping to return to its original bed. Nana sat beside me and watched Father as he stalked throughout the room, rubbing his shoes over the tiny depressions left in the rug by the legs of the rearranged chairs. My older brother sat by the banister and took apart an old, broken watch—one of the many little mechanical things he kept in his pockets as part of his constant, relentless search for the heart of the inanimate world. He was not so successful, however, in putting things back together, and he had long ago learned to keep his hands off our parents' belongings.

We heard a car stop in front of the house and Nana was at once by the window. I followed, my brother behind me stuffing the shambles of the watch back into his pocket. Father remained by the fireplace, adjusting a doily that was too small for the table he'd placed it on the night before. It was the taxi. Mother got out first, then Grandad. I first noticed his hands: they were too large for his body. Then out jumped a little white dog so covered with fur I couldn't tell where it began or ended. The cab drove off at once. Grandad walked slowly toward our house, his enormous right hand swallowing the handle of his cane while his dog ran in frantic circles around his legs. Mother, loaded down with suitcases, struggled through the front door and immediately bumped into a chair that had been across the room only a day ago. Father said, "You didn't say anything about a dog." Grandad entered, clamped an outrageous hand over Father's, and shook it, saying, "Good to be here, Bob. You seem to have grown a bit since I last saw you." I then noticed he was taller than Father. I knew that elderly people shrank, but Grandad looked as though he'd grown instead, and in my imagination his huge hands were a presage of what he might become. I began to understand why I had never met Grandad earlier.

Before Mother began the formal greetings Nana had already welcomed him and after a quick nod of her head disappeared with the luggage. My brother barely noticed Grandad, his eyes instead fixed on the dog that still raced in circles: he was sure it was a mechanical toy. I refused to shake Grandad's hand, afraid it would devour my own. He laughed and said, "Shy, eh? That's all right, you'll get to know me well enough." Then while Mother quietly but seriously questioned Father about the changed plan of the house I was struck sharply on the ankle by a cane. I turned around, my impulse to cry out stifled by Grandad's smiling stare and his hand patting my head and slopping over it like an extra-large cap. Grandad stopped abruptly at the sound of his dog's yelp. We all turned to see it licking its tail while my brother shuffled his guilty foot. "It was an accident," he said, his eyes filled with sadness at the sight of the injured, nonmechanical dog. Mother finally led Grandad up the stairs to the guest room, her hand at his elbow but not actually touching it. He was strong and only pretended to need help, and Mother only pretended to help him.

My brother and I returned to our bedroom, struck silent when we once again regarded how Father had reversed our sides of the room the night before. My brother's side, now on the right, was as usual a catastrophe, a ruined plain of dismembered toy guns, gutted clocks, and cheap, broken cameras. The internal workings of his closet's doorknob were scattered on the floor, along with crooked minute and second hands, shattered lens covers, and plastic triggers. In the middle of it all was a bicycle wheel, the spokes twisted in every direction like a field of wheat exposed to conflicting winds. My own side of the room, now on the left, seemed empty. All of my possessions were carefully placed out of sight, in my closet, toy chest, and drawers, away from any opportunity of tempting my brother. Yet when even these precautions failed, I had a form of revenge—necessarily indirect because my brother was much bigger than I. He was ticklish. If I found one of my toys destroyed on the floor, I waited until night. Once he was asleep I rose, walked across the room, and tickled him as gently as possible until his body was one quivering mass that shook long after I returned to my bed. There I listened to him giggling in a kind of half-sleep. I knew he would wake in the morning exhausted, with a confused look on his face. As my brother and I tried to accustom ourselves to our transposed room we could hear Grandad settling into the guest room down the hall. My brother's gaze kept returning to my new side of the room, and I nervously opened my toy chest filled with books and stared at their shining covers.

That afternoon Mother went through all the rearranged rooms, searching for her houseplants. She had every imaginable variety: dog tail cactus that slowly died in a sandy bed, immune to tending; long creeping string-of-hearts that grew faster than she could trim them; brittle jade succulents whose leaves snapped off at the slightest touch; replanted sprays and shoots of lipstick and prayer plants that flourished without water. Mother acquired her plants by the beauty of their names, not out of any practical considerations: false aralias, weeping figs, and umbrella plants were placed together without thought of compatibility of sunlight or moisture; maidenhair ferns, flame violets, and piggyback and mother-of-thousands plants lined up together like a sexual litany, sharing the same relentless exposure. Yet Mother worked hard at them all, ignoring the fact that the plants grew, withered, died, or regenerated without her consent.

Now that Father had moved the furniture and the plants they displayed, her problems were multiplied. Baby's tears were sent a room away from Moses-in-the-cradle. A snake plant no longer curled near lady's-eardrops. Mother began new arrangements in the wake of Father's. She resettled her plants as best she could without daring, even by the simple movement of a single chair, to overrule her husband's alterations. She must have known that his energy for interior decorating, if arrested, would turn on Grandad. Father, smoking a cigarette on the second-floor landing, watched Mother's attempts ruefully, yet also with satisfaction: he saw that his changes bred more changes. And so my parents' efforts at order circled each other throughout the house, forming a larger pattern of their quiet moments together. For I had seen them more than once when they thought they were alone, sitting together without talking, without looking at each other, without even staring off in the same direction. Their hands had met at the table, their fingers containing and then contained in the palm of the other, in an absentminded and futile search for a firm clasp.

His first day with us Grandad made himself at home. I sat on the sofa of the living room, a book on my lap about a baker whose loaves wouldn't stop rising, and watched as Grandad counted everything in the room. He started with a single object, an ashtray, and slowly made a circuit among the furniture. With each whispered number he touched another ashtray, as if the pressing of his large hand upon it made it his own. Once he was done with the ashtrays he started on the lamps, the chairs, the statuary, continuing until he exhausted every possession in the room. All the while his dog endlessly looped around his legs like a little living top. Surfeited, finally, from all this addition, Grandad went for an afternoon walk. When he returned he sat in an armchair and fell asleep. Grandad's lips moved while he napped, and I imagined that he was counting whatever was in his dreams. At his feet slept the dog, turning a slow and careful circle around the legs of its master. Mother, visible through the open door of the kitchen, seemed not to notice Grandad's behavior. She was too busy marking with a red pen a copy of *Houseplants: Their Joys and Sorrows.* Her worried face rose briefly when I sat down at the table across from her. I smiled, she smiled, and then she turned once more to her book.

As the days passed Father continued to shift the furniture in our house, always in the middle of the night. But Father's response was backfiring. Grandad enjoyed the constant new groupings. He woke each morning to a fresh slate for more of his incessant counting, as if he were keeping time to a song that wouldn't stop playing inside him. He even counted the steps on the way up to the second floor and the rungs of the banister on the way down. The only time I saw him stop was to listen when Nana sang in the shower upstairs.

Meanwhile, our changing house was beginning to affect my brother. Here was a kind of magic: Father could take apart a room *without breaking it,* and without trying to put it back together there was created *another room.* In the face of this, my brother's failures with every sort of mechanical object began to disturb him. Late at night he listened carefully to Father's footsteps and the muffled groans of furniture, and he tried to decipher the unseen changes. He heard the silence come apart, yet when Father was done, the quiet healed itself and returned without revealing any secrets. It was then that my brother tugged at my foot in the dark and left the bedroom. This was a challenge to a game of hide-and-seek. I followed. Down in the living room we kept as silent as possible, so as not to disturb the rest of the family. We prowled among unfamiliar arrangements of furniture we could barely see, and at times the darkness took shape and bumped into us as we crept about on the abundant quiet of the rug.

One night I woke to hear my brother taking apart his bed frame, loosening the springs one by one, as if he were trying to find some lost moving part of an interrupted dream. Before he could begin to dissect his mattress I walked over and touched his shoulder. "Go to sleep," I whispered, and he did. In the morning he woke up startled at the surrounding wreck of his bed. Father passed by our room on his way downstairs and glanced in. Without a word he left and returned with a handful of tools. He repaired the bed silently, somehow understanding his son's impulse. My brother watched tight-lipped from a corner, obviously blaming his misery on Father. When the bed was rebuilt I asked Father to juggle for us. He picked up some old, crushed Ping-Pong balls, but his mind was elsewhere as he twirled them in the air. He gazed, sighing, at the dresser and chairs in our room, perhaps wishing they too could be tossed about with ease.

Downstairs, Grandad counted, all the while moving among the furniture. Nana carefully kept out of his reach, as though afraid one of his enormous hands would shoot out and grab her, and she would then be counted along with everything else in the room. When Grandad thought no one was watching he stared at Nana while she avoided him. I could see, even from the second-floor landing, that he was attracted to her. Perhaps he saw in her quickness a superior version of his restless, circling dog—Nana, after all, could move in a straight line. But she was surely secondary in his affections: what Grandad loved was our house. The changing landscape of the rooms plus the unpredictable proliferation and dying out of houseplants, which moved throughout the house in counterpoint to the furniture, provided him with endless possibilities of counting. With Nana on his side he just might be able to stay for good. From then on, when his lips moved during his naps I was sure he was counting the days he had left in his summer's visit, days filled with plots on Nana's heart.

He came up to me one day while I was reading a book about a wonderful machine that manufactured empty dreams, waiting to be filled, and he said, "Your grandmother is a fine woman, a *fine* woman. Tell me, what little present can I give her that she'd like?"

"Candy," I said without hesitation.

"Thank you, m'boy," he replied, patting his hand over my head as if I were his odious dog.

Nana hated sweets. She blamed them for her false teeth. Whenever she caught me or my brother eating a piece of licorice or chocolate she would begin a lecture that ended in our laughter and her chasing us through the house, her false teeth out and snapping in her hand, but chasing us just slowly enough that we could get away. My brother always ran with reluctance, his eyes on her teeth: he would have loved to take them apart.

Grandad returned from his next afternoon walk with a candy sampler box. It was almost lost in the vast plain of his palm as he presented it to Nana.

"What's this?" she asked.

"A present . . . for you."

"Candy? For me?" She stared at him. Finally she said, "Thank you very much," and took out her false teeth. With them she deftly picked up the sampler box from his hand and walked away. Grandad didn't move. Even his dog stopped in mid-circuit, panting. I slumped down in my chair behind a book of riddles—*What is a house without any doors? . . . An egg*—and tried to keep from giggling.

After that I was always careful to stay out of range of Grandad's cane: I formed a larger, invisible circle around him that echoed the endless arcs of his dog. I hated that animal, and it was my job to walk it every morning. If no one was watching I snapped the collar around its waist rather than struggle through the fur to find its head. Then I pulled it sideways out the front door and walked as fast as I could, dragging it along while it tried to run in small circles behind me. One day after walking the dog I returned to discover that one of my favorite books, an old volume of Nordic folktales, was strewn about on my bedroom floor. The strings of binding were in one corner, the heavy embossed cover in another, and scattered everywhere else were page after page of beautifully illustrated dragons, talking trees, and gnomes hiding among snowy landscapes. My brother was gone, and he didn't return until just before dinner.

"I can put it all back together," he said to me at once. "I promise. Look, I bought a magnifying glass so I can do it." He displayed the glass before his guilty face, his eyes curiously enlarged and distorted. I said nothing, knowing that this new toy would be in pieces long before he turned to repairing my book. With bitterness I went back to watching the evening meal being prepared.

Nana always helped Mother in the kitchen but moved so fast that she was always ahead of her. Mother found herself giving directions that had already been carried out. The refrigerator door was open before she could ask for the potatoes. Nana had washed the lettuce before Mother said, while opening a package of frozen peas, "I think a salad would be perfect with the meal." Mother sat down to dinner, as she did every night, with a bewildered look on her face, trying as she ate to reconstruct the elusive decisions of the meal's preparation. Nana sat patiently in front of her cleaned plate, waiting for the rest of us to finish. My brother studied the internal structure of the cherry tomato as he carefully picked out the little seeds with his fork and then tried, in vain, to put it all back together. Father directed the passing of the plates on the table so that whatever Grandad needed would be out of his reach. Grandad, whenever he could get hold of a serving plate, counted: the peas, the fries, the number of pieces he cut from his meat. As he ate, he subtracted, all the while his fantastic hands swallowing up his knife and fork. I watched everyone else and as usual I was the last to finish.

I waited for my brother to fall asleep that night so I could tickle him as he'd never been tickled before. But he stayed awake for hours, listening to the moving of furniture downstairs. I must have dozed off while I waited, because suddenly I was aware that quiet had settled over the house. I rose and crossed to my brother's bedside. He was gone. I knew he had to be downstairs, exploring for ever elusive clues of reconstruction in Father's latest revision of the rooms. Drawn by my brother's obsession I followed down to the darkness, where I immediately bumped into a floor lamp. I held it fast but it continued to rattle from the jolt. My brother then knew I was in the living room, and where, and so I found myself in the middle of a game of hide-and-seek.

With caution I began to slink along on the rug, not sure who was seeking whom. I edged past an ottoman and a sofa, my hand out before me, testing the darkness with a light touch. When I crept by a large potted fig tree I heard breathing. It was my brother approaching from the other direction. I was about to tag him, but stopped: I heard Grandad's dog panting and banging into the banister as it ran in circles down the steps. I knew that in the center of that orbit was Grandad. Soon I heard him counting in a whisper the furniture his dog was running into, but I knew he was looking for me. His cane began to skit across wide stretches of rug—searching, I was sure, for an exposed elbow, knee, or tender forehead. Yet here also was my moment of revenge. I turned and tickled my brother in the darkness and through his surprise all he could do was crouch there, holding back shrieks of laughter as Grandad's cane swept along inches from us. I left him with his silent, teary convulsions and retraced my passage to the stairs, easily avoiding Grandad and his dog. Once in the bedroom I quietly closed the door. This marked the beginning of a long estrangement between my brother and me.

I thought I'd finished off Grandad's hopes, but he counterattacked. In the late afternoons when he woke from his nap, he began to hum and whistle songs I was sure were very old. They seemed like the same melodies Nana attempted in the shower, but Grandad's versions sounded clean and clear, as if scrubbed dry with a towel. While his cane tapped out a lively rhythm his dog yawned from its nap in small breaths of sudden harmony. At first, Nana came in from the kitchen and vaguely listened as she fluffed the couch pillows. In the days that followed she managed to find *something* to do in the living room when Grandad started his informal concerts, even if it was cleaning ashtrays that hadn't yet been used. Eventually she just sat in a nearby chair, as motionless as I'd ever seen her, and she looked out a window that shone with the light of the setting sun. Before long others began to suspect what I had long known of Grandad's intentions. My brother, sensing an attachment was forming, watched attentively, as if in glances and significant silences he could make out moving parts fitting together. Mother stopped watering her plants, her suspicions stunning her into inaction. Her plants flourished without her, and dark patches of winding green soon took over the corners of the house. Father, however, continued his switching of tables and chairs, incapable of discovering the unthinkable.

Meanwhile, Nana was becoming slower and slower. Once she chased my brother and me for our parents but we slipped easily from the grasp of her fingers. She may have been slowed down by the creeping tendrils on the rug; in any case, we eventually let her catch us. As Nana grew slower, Father's moving obsession increased. At night we could hear him finishing the entire first-floor rearrangement in just a few minutes. It was at this time that he began switching the contents of the kitchen closets. In the morning Mother would open the cupboards to find the meat tenderizer beside the whole-wheat bread, the coffee cups with the roasted peanuts, as she looked for the cereal. My brother sulked while he ate, knowing that each simple meal placed before him had been put together after an elaborate series of searches. Mother grew more confused than ever at mealtimes, unaccustomed to the impossible combinations in her cabinets, unaccustomed to the sudden absence of Nana's uncanny cooking intuitions. For Nana was now the last to come to the table and the last to finish eating. Her plate would still be full as she watched Grandad count the last of his buttered carrots. One night I passed her on the way to the sink with the dirty dishes: on her breath was the unmistakable scent of chocolate.

During one of Grandad's afternoon concerts, at the end of a syncopated melody, he placed his fat hand over one of Nana's and his lips silently counted, "One." Then he started to hum a new tune. I sat across from both of them in amazement and my book—about an Indian who tried to live the future he'd painted on his face before it faded away—dropped to the floor, bouncing close to Grandad's dog. It growled at me with a wavery rasp that spiraled in its throat. Nana, lost in a song that itself was lost in another age, noticed none of this. I saw that Nana would only be saved if she started moving again, if she gathered the speed that would place her out of Grandad's reach.

But no one could help, that much I understood about them all: while I didn't know why they all did what they did, I knew that they would keep on doing it.

It was in frustration that I crept down to the living room that night, to feel in the dark Father's latest changes. I pressed my hands against the smoothness of the uphol-stered chairs, the coldness of the glass coffee table, while my brother watched me from the top of the stairs. Something in the furniture seemed to yield, slightly, to my touch. I soon found myself, as best my small body could manage, returning everything to its original position of the evening. Lush green creepers twisted beneath my feet. My brother, his eyes accustomed to the dark, remained where he was, unbelieving, as I put the entire room back together again. It was a humiliation I hadn't planned, a humiliation that at first left him immobile. He must have seen my feat as a challenge that asked for an even more daring attempt. As I continued to push and sweat in the dark he rose and walked down the second-floor hallway. Then he opened the door to Nana's bedroom. Once there, he should have easily made out Nana's false teeth at rest in a glass of water.

He must have given up in the early morning. I imagine him slowly gathering from the rug a litter of artificial teeth and dropping them, one by one, back into the glass of water—a series of impossible wishes—only holding the last tooth back, his final admission of defeat. That must have been what he held in his hand back in our room as he turned restlessly in bed.

I rose early to survey my rewriting of the living room's history. My brother followed me, one fist clenched, his forehead sweating. I nervously watched him pacing around the room. Father walked down the stairs a half hour later. At first he didn't realize anything was different. But when he absentmindedly flicked his cigarette ash not into an ashtray but onto the armrest of the couch, he suddenly stopped. Only his eyes moved, taking in a room that somehow hadn't changed. Grandad came down the stairs, his lips quivering with incipient counting, and stopped when he too noticed the unchanged aspect of the room. No new landscapes to count. He stood next to Father, staring: two enemies joined for a moment in their separate disappointments. Mother came down next and looked in surprise at Grandad and Father standing so closely and peacefully together. Nana was the last to appear, with a slow and deliberate walk. She was holding something in her hands and her lips moved involuntarily. She made straight for Grandad and opened her hands in front of his face, revealing the broken remains of her false teeth.

"You—this is your fault! You and your *chocolates*!" she screamed in a voice that mixed rage with the wheeze of a gutted mouth. She grabbed one of Grandad's hands and dropped the teeth in his huge palm.

"I-I d-don't know what you mean, m'dear," Grandad stuttered. He stared at the teeth in amazement. His other hand beat his cane nervously on the floor.

"You know, you *do* know!" Nana's face was now dark with unspeakable possibilities. We were all silent. Grandad continued tapping his cane—which must have been in rhythm with all our heartbeats—and his dog did a high-strung dance around it. Nana impulsively grabbed the cane and, with a strength none of us suspected, snapped it in two and threw it on the floor. My brother, by now almost feverish, lost all sense of discretion and rushed toward this new broken object in need of repair. In so doing he dropped the single tooth he had been gripping in his fist. We all saw this, and then we all knew.

Nana lunged at my brother. Still slow, she missed, and

he slipped behind a large hanging plant. She rushed at him again as he ran out the door, hopping over vines that wove across the floor by the foyer. Mother, after watching helplessly, ran outside after Nana, as much to defend her son from physical harm as to finally grab hold of events. As usual she was doomed to failure: Grandad's spell of the past few weeks was broken, and Nana was picking up speed and gaining on my brother. Father ran after Mother, finally defending Nana now that she no longer needed help, but he was mostly impelled by his frustrated rearranging. As he sped away from Grandad he stepped on the dog's paw. It yelped and, unhinged by all the excitement, tore after Father, snapping at his feet and growling its dizzy growl. I leapt after that hated beast but it ran ahead in a rapid series of circles like a tiny, horizontal tornado. Grandad then staggered after me as fast as he could without his cane. I turned my head back a moment and saw him, somehow triumphant in his defeat, *counting,* counting us all as we chased each other in an angry ragged line from our deserted house.

VI

The Art of the Knock:
Three

While I wait for my first patient to appear, I think back to when, as a young boy alone in my room at night, with the entire world outside frighteningly quiet, I dreamt of a huge wooden door with the faces of my parents carved above its heavy iron lock. When I tugged and pulled at the knob, its dark surface only reflected my unhappy hands. I woke up crying, my small fists clutching air, but my mother and father, always sound sleepers, never came to my bedside. Those nightmares continued and grew with me throughout my childhood: I dreamt of a pine door that wept its resin at my approach until my shoes stuck me to the sidewalk just out of the range of knocking; I dreamt of a home's smoldering facade and its burnt and crumpled door, which only partially revealed the ghastly interior. I always woke up knowing that I was trapped, not inside but *outside,* and what lay behind the doors always remained a sullen mystery.

And so I tried to knuckle my way through life, as a salesman, as a mailman, hoping there was something in my pounding that would make every door swing free. But how could my hands hope to successfully rage against such a solid refusal? No, after years of attempted roughhouse, I decided to abandon the failure of my hands and instead use my brain, that hidden fist of ingenuity. And today I attribute the success of my psychiatric practice to my early preoccupations, for only by looking into my past could I finally see my future.

There were numerous specialty therapies I might have embraced at the beginning of my career. I *was* tempted to use the amplified megaphone for the Primal Whisper, and the knot manual for String Therapy. Other, even more specific techniques had their attractions, such as the cookie cutter collection of human shapes for curing anorexic patients, so they can be tempted to bake and then eat the family member of their choice. I briefly considered the Free-Association Water Bucket, used for patients' reflections and which the doctor can kick at any time during the session for a new therapeutic ripple, and the Pinball Machine with flashing Rorschach blots, with its extra-point system for a free session and its secret tilt button. Yet now, when five or six of my colleagues and I occasionally gather together to drink and chat and covet each other's particular methods, nothing, I think, approaches the professional jealousy that is felt for my own special practice.

Perhaps this is so because I never meet my patients. My revolutionizing of the doctor-patient relationship comes from my realization that therapy, like life, is a door that must be beaten upon. Our skins are thin lies hiding a world of marrow and bone, dreams and nightmares, and what better way to reveal that interior than through the outposts of the fists? Every session, one of my patients stands in the waiting room and knocks on my office door, which is made of the finest wood. Carved on it are the words

KNOCK

THE DOCTOR
IS LISTENING

I sit inside, as if I were in a confessional. Of course, I never open the door: why interrupt my patient's progress? Besides, it's my role to hear each nuance of personality in every tap and telling blow, every tumbling tone of the fingertips. I *know* the knock, and to me its wishes and hidden histories are as revealing as any stutter or slip of the tongue. And the voice itself is like the knock, the tongue raging against the prison of the mouth, the lips pursing their lengths together into sound like fingers forming into gesture. For what *are* words but the products of inner pounding? The blade of the tongue flicks against the palate, its tip touching the teeth, releasing consonants like an explosion, letting vowels slip out through rounded lips.

So I sit in my office each morning and wait for my first patient of the day to begin knocking. Today it's the young man who longs for the lost memory of his birth. As usual, he arrives a bit early—he was, after all, a premature baby. He taps quickly at the beginning of the session, trying to capture the nervous heartbeat of the birth trauma. I carefully note the skips in rhythm, always significant, I believe, in revealing ambivalence toward the mother. Then comes the measured, almost bell-like pounding: his response to the doctors and nurses and the mythic position they hold in his unconscious. As none of this knocking seems to work, instead he now taps out his pride at the stroller he recently built for himself, and of his happiness when he pushes it down the street with his framed baby picture propped up on the lace pillows. He finally knocks good-bye, pounding like the wooden sighs and creaks of the cradle, and then he squeaks his palms down the length of the door: the sound of a distant, crying infant.

I immediately recognize the knock of my next patient— the young woman who carries an obsession with her father in every finger and tries to shake it out on my office door. Each one of her knuckles contains a knot of bitterness, memories made raw by her insistent touch. Today she bangs away her anger at the game her father played with her when she was a child: Underwater Adventure. He would hold her face in the sink and then slowly count the bubbles as her breath ran out, and with each dunking he tried for a new record. As she pounds out this tale her fists sound like the breaking of bubbles on the surface of the water, bursts of disillusionment. This time she doesn't come up for air until the end of our session, a new record. She leaves and I make a few notes—"This transference should be good for at least five more sessions"—and await the next patient.

A few tentative taps: it's the husband who can't remember his wife's name. Nothing works. He's even tattooed it on his body, but now he can't remember where, and he's ashamed, of course, to undress in public to check. In our sessions he pounds through the alphabet in Morse code: today we're on *N*. Nadia, Nancy, Nanette, Naomi, Nell? Netty, Nicolette, Nina, Nora, Norma? No luck again. He finally stops at Nyssa. He tries to hammer out the passionate details of his letters to her during their courtship; he even attempts to untap their long-ago twisting on her absent parents' sofa. But whenever he comes close to recalling a revealing, luminous moment, his fists just *graze* the office door: suddenly he's a shower of sideswipes and the memory is lost. So he returns to the present, thumping his dilemma. Every day he phones across town to where his wife works. Tongue-tied when she answers, he hangs up, and later during dinner she complains about the crank caller. When his session is over he knocks farewell, but when he comes to my name, his hands stutter into silence.

And so my day continues. Finally, I'm listening to my last patient, the old woman who wants to elope with her grandson. She pounds out fantastic genealogical tables to establish that they're really not related, but soon her contradictory evidence reduces her to fists of sobbing. Eventually her fingertips detail his endearing features: his two temporarily missing front teeth, his delightful lisp, the colorful scrapes of his knees and elbows, and the incipient bulge of his shorts. Then she flurries out solid proof of her potential as a helpmeet: her long-standing knowledge of nursery rhymes, her encyclopedic understanding of the rules of children's games, and also how she is slowly shrinking down through age to the size to which her grandson is growing. *Would you be best man?* she raps to me, but I withhold my RSVP, remaining silent, and soon I hear her leave, the echoes of her tapping cane slowly diminishing.

It's late afternoon, I'm tired of my door's reverberations, and my hands have broken out in a sympathetic rash. It's time to go home. I drive through the city's side streets slowly, my doors locked and my windows up, and I watch the silent brownstone faces as I pass by. Lights begin to go on inside them while the sun sets, and I leave them behind. By evening I'm home, at the long end of my country lane, and that large building might just as well be another shadow at the edge of the wooded fields. Once inside, I bolt the door and lead myself through a path of light as I flip the switches in the halls and rooms that I enter. After the simple meal I make myself for dinner, I stare at the paneled walls. There should be mail in the box outside, but I don't care to listen to the squeak of its little metal door. Instead, I slowly prepare myself for bed and the inevitable nightmare that recurs almost as soon as I fall asleep.

I dream that my hands have passed away. I'm standing in a corner at the funeral, unrecognized, my stumps in my pockets, and I watch helplessly as the mourners line up at the casket for a last handshake. Then they give the coffin a knock for good luck. When everyone is done, they applaud. I remain alone, quiet. The pallbearers come and we follow them to the cemetery, to the tiny grave that has already been dug. After the coffin is lowered in, everyone throws a handful of dirt on its top. Finally we leave, the others turning in their own time for a final wave goodbye. I walk beside them, the ends of my wrists itching.

My hands wake up in the coffin: they're still alive! Restless and uncertain, they crawl around the edges of the cramped walls until they finally realize where they are and clutch each other in fear. This, slowly, turns into a wrestling match, the two hands grappling over the coffin's satin cushion. Equally matched, they stop, and then together, plank by plank, they begin to pry themselves out of their prison. But once out, they're lost underground and begin to dig a tunnel in no specific direction, knowing only that at the end of it they will find me.

Through the solid, resistant dark, they eventually come upon a tree, first a single root, then the whole tangle of its system. They're uncertain of what they've found. Following the length of each root, they test to see if it's an arm and, at the tip and taking turns, they seek to reattach themselves to what they think is the wrist, hoping to finally find a home. When they discover all of the tips to be frauds, they're enraged by such an intricate betrayal. Just as methodically as before, they then grip the roots and slowly throttle them. And so, aboveground a thin line of dead trees appears, advancing through the forest like a single-minded plague.

Meanwhile, I'm at the concert hall. The orchestra is winding up my favorite symphony—Beethoven's Seventh. Refusing to sit by helpless, the raw ends of my wrists si-

lent on either side of my tuxedo while the rest of the audience applauds, I pack my program and leave before the last few bars. I reach the lobby just as the crowd goes wild. Back in the auditorium, fingers break through the floor under my abandoned seat: my hands have just missed me. They reach for the carpeted edge and pull themselves up. They can't understand it: I'm not there! In their confusion, they begin to applaud along with everyone else around them, slowly at first, not knowing why.

They arrive early the next morning at my office, a quarter hour before my first expected patient. I sit inside, my rounded wrists lying on my lap, and then I begin to hear knocking. . . .

I wake up, sweaty and frightened: Do I still have my hands? I think desperately. I flail against the black air and feel nothing, until the fingernails of my clenched hands cut into my palms. While I'm relieved by the pain, surrounded now by the dim forms of furniture in the room, I continue on my back in bed to punch the air above, though there's no surface to knock, no wooden grain to greet me. "Open up! Open up!" I scream in the middle of the night, at the millions of hidden doors in the dark.

VII

China

After our last calendar was smudged into a black wing, long after our watches had lost track of all those passed minutes, only then did we begin to fear our tunnel might actually reach to the other side, to China.

The dark walls had come to be a comfort, a close sky that rose and set in a circle around us. The tunnel face too: we were constantly digging into the unknown and it was always familiar. Until one day, our shovels long gone, we found our hands fist-full of a soft, rich loam, finely traced with roots.

We stopped and sat together. Neither of us wanted to face the truth: that the task itself had become our destination, which was both at hand and distant, a comfort and a challenge. That this should end was a possibility we had ceased to consider. Our silence was broken by a foot that crashed through our tunnel face, along with its owner's shout. In the end, it was China that came to us.

We helped the foot back to the surface. The end of our tunnel now just a hole, we looked up with dirty faces at a curious crowd looking down at us. We waved and tried to smile. We'd long since forgotten our Arrival Speech, lost our notes, and misplaced the very language of the home we'd left behind. We merely lengthened our waving into a gesture, understandable even to foreigners, of *Please, help lift us up*.

We were soon surrounded by Chinese of all ages, touching our earth-caked clothes and faces, jabbering in their own exotic dialects. We blinked and shielded our eyes from the terribly bright sun. Then slowly, by a kind of communal push and pull, we were being led away to a nearby city. As we reached the outskirts we caught our first glimpse of those celebrated wall posters. They seemed to be everywhere, with a simple, oddly familiar calligraphy and decorated with illustrations: here a tube of toothpaste, there a set of radial tires. It was then I noticed that the children following us were chewing gum and blowing large, unpleasant bubbles.

After a mile or so of posters we felt slightly bitter. Had we left our home so far behind only to be reminded of it here? Where were the rice paddies, the pagodas; why so many automobiles instead of bicycles? But worst, and most suspicious, why was the language so easy to understand—had we imagined it so successfully that we had somehow learned it? *Could* we, indeed, read the calligraphy, or were our translations merely lucky guesses?

Possessed of a desperate fear, I finally turned to grab one of our companions and hold his face close to mine: to feel the fold of skin above the eye, to touch the flattened nose. But he backed off, as did everyone else and, frightened by my anger, the crowd dispersed until their features were blurred by distance.

We were now in the city, alone, with traffic all around us. Horns honked from every direction and we just stood there in the middle of the street. Then we looked away from each other, both of us unwilling to say what we feared: that perhaps we had dug a U-shaped tunnel that carried us back to the beginning. And yet, could it be instead that our eyes, at first unaccustomed to the light, were still unaccustomed to China? We stood there, concentrating, and then didn't that tall building across from us have the graceful features of a pagoda, wasn't everyone passing by dressed in silk robes? The storefronts were filled with landscape scrolls and tea sets; the smell of watercress was in the air. Above the din of traffic we were sure we could hear, from all the open windows, the steady click of chopsticks. We looked all around us: not a blonde in sight! Satisfied, we began to walk across the street, dodging a bus, a speeding cab. Of all the different Chinas we had dreamt of or imagined on our journey, we were ready for the one we were in now.

A Note About the Author

Philip Graham has worked as a carpenter, bartender, cab driver, upholsterer's apprentice, staysail-ship crew member, and Santa Claus. He has taught creative writing in Virginia, New York, and Pennsylvania, and is currently an assistant professor of English at Southern Illinois University. A MacDowell Colony Fellow and the recipient of an Illinois Arts Council grant, he has published his work in *The New Yorker*, *The Paris Review*, *Virginia Quarterly Review*, *Mid-American Review*, and many other magazines. He lives with his wife, Alma Gottlieb, a cultural anthropologist.